PURSUED

Raider Warlords of the Vandar #4

TANA STONE

Broadmoor Books

CHAPTER ONE

Alana

I leaned against the steel hull of the ship as the imperial soldiers rolled metal crates of cargo up the ramp and coughed as a gust kicked up dust around me. For a moment, I wondered what was in the locked containers stamped with foreign symbols. Then I remembered that it didn't matter, and I didn't care. The cargo wasn't the point of my mission, and whatever had been placed inside the crates I'd be transporting was only there to hide the trackers. Trackers that would lead the Zagrath to the Vandar horde I was planning to infiltrate.

The idea of going solo into a Vandar horde should have terrified me. It would have made any reasonable person's blood run cold. But I wasn't a reasonable person. I was one of the empire's top assassins. I was the one they sent in when they needed someone fearless. Someone who wasn't afraid to kill or be killed. The one who seduced her victims before she killed them. The one they called Mantis in dark whispers.

Flicking my fingers through the choppy layers of hair that brushed my shoulders, I scanned the outpost's crowded shipyard and sighed. Despite the fact that I was heading out for my most deadly mission yet, I was eager to get off the planet. The time between missions always made me antsy. I'd rather be in the thick of a battle or deep undercover than waiting. Waiting gave me too much time to think, and thinking too much was never a good thing in my line of work. I tapped one of my black boots on the ground. Not to mention the fact that patience was not one of my virtues, especially not if it meant hanging out on a backwater outpost for much longer.

I took a bite of the hard jerky I'd been nibbling on—my sad excuse for breakfast—the salty flavor sharp on my tongue. Swallowing, I gazed at the buildings in the distance.

Rellaren looked like any other imperial outpost, with Zagrath soldiers in steel-blue uniforms and shiny, black helmets bustling around dull-gray ships. Gleaming droids zoomed across the hardpacked earth, dodging the faceless soldiers and emitting sharp beeps. Ships arrived and departed with regularity, kicking up clouds of dust that made me pull my shirt over my nose to keep from choking.

"Another day in paradise," I muttered to myself.

Like most imperial outposts, Rellaren had barracks for soldiers as well as rowdy canteens for the couriers and supply runners to occupy their time while they waited for cargo to be loaded and unloaded. Repair shops were pressed up against scrap-metal dealers, and an open-air market sold you just about anything you could need for a space journey. There were a few discreet pleasure houses on the outskirts, but the quality of the pleasurers was not what you'd find on a pleasure planet or a pleasure ship. Not that I frequented pleasure houses, but I heard enough of the other crews talking to know.

Even from a distance, the scent of greasy food being prepared for the midday meal mixed with fumes from the engines, making the air around me both hazy and fetid. I glanced at the soldiers still wheeling crates into the belly of my ship. I should have time for a last Rellaren *menashi*. The thin bread spread with a spiced meat paste and wrapped into a long roll was the only redeeming quality of the dingy outpost. My stomach growled as I thought about the crunch of the bread and the tangy kick of the meat. Since I'd be eating ration packs on the ship until I was intercepted by the Vandar, this was my last chance for decent food.

Before I could head for the nearest *menashi* stand outside the gates of the shipyard, a hand closed over my arm. Without thinking, I clamped my own hand on top and spun around, flipping the male onto his back and landing on top of him with my knees straddling his shoulders.

"Whoa, Alana." The Rellarian male's eyes were wide as he blinked up at me. "I just came to see you off."

I leaned back and released my grip on his hands. "You shouldn't sneak up on me like that, Tannel."

The creases in his brow relaxed, leaving only the traditional Rellarian ridges that formed a point between his eyebrows. "Not that I mind you being on top."

I gave him a half smile as I stood and pulled him up with me. Even though Tannel was taller and broader than me, he didn't have the years of combat training I did—or the finely honed reflexes. "Maybe next visit."

He closed the short distance between us, lowering his head to mine. His light-brown hair tickled my cheek as it fell forward. "You sure you have to rush off so soon? You just got here."

I shrugged and tried to ignore the warmth of his breath on my neck. "Sorry. The life of an imperial supply runner."

He gave a snort of laughter. "You're the finest imperial supply runner I've ever seen."

"You mean I'm the only one you share your bed with?" I teased.

Another laugh, this one louder. "You clearly haven't seen your competition. Big, hairy Taralians. Grulnix with spikes for hands. No, I'll take a Zagrath like you any day."

"I'm not Zagrath," I corrected. I'd had that fact pounded into me enough that my reaction was automatic.

"Human, then. Didn't the Zagrath and humans both come from Earth?"

"A long time ago. The Zagrath were the ones with the money and resources to augment their biology. That's why they're bigger."

He put a hand on my waist. "I still prefer your biology."

"Yeah?" I tried to keep the bitterness out of my voice. "Well, the Zagrath also live longer than humans do."

"And rule the galaxy," Tannel grumbled, then caught himself. "Not that I mean I don't—"

"I'm not going to turn you in." I lowered my voice so the passing soldiers couldn't hear me. "I know not everyone likes living under imperial rule."

He let out a relieved breath. "So, why do you work for them again?"

"The same reason you live on one of their outposts."

He cocked his head at me. "You have no choice."

"Does anyone have a choice when it comes to the Empire?" I asked. "At least they pay well."

"For supply runners, maybe. Not if you run a repair shop." Tannel peered up at my ship. "When are you going to take me with you?"

I stifled a sigh. As much as I enjoyed my time spent rolling around in bed with the Rellarian, I could never take him with me. For all he knew, I delivered supplies from one imperial planet to the next. He had no clue that I left a trail of dead imperial enemies in my wake. I had a feeling it would sour our relationship if he knew I could snap his neck in a matter of seconds.

"Come on," I slapped at his chest. "You'd miss all this. There are no *menashi* in space."

He held my gaze. "But you're there."

Oh, boy. I did my best to keep things casual with the males I used for release and entertainment. I kept it fun and fast, and was always clear from the start that I didn't want anything serious. In my line of work, I couldn't risk getting attached to anyone or anything. Not when an attachment could be used against me. And I could *not* allow myself to have any weaknesses. Not if I was the best. And I had to be the best. The empire had also drilled *that* into me.

I stood on my tiptoes and kissed him lightly. "I promise to do something extra special to you next time."

The hurt expression behind his eyes faded, and his vertical, almond-shaped pupils flared. "You sure you don't have time now?" His hand tightened on my waist, and he jerked me against him. "I can give you something to think about while you're gone."

The bulge in his pants was hard as it pressed into my stomach, and I wished I did have time. The Rellarian might not be the sharpest blade, but what he didn't have in brains he made up for with the size of his cock, and he was my favorite distraction on the outpost. Even more than *menashi*, and that was saying something.

I cut my eyes to the imperial soldiers loading my ship. Their helmets made it impossible to tell if they were watching me, but I shouldn't take any chances. I stepped away from Tannel. "Next time. I promise."

He frowned. "How long will you be gone?"

"No idea." This wasn't a lie. My mission could be quick, or it could take so long he'd forget all about me. I had no illusions that the Rellarian was faithful to me, nor did I want him to be.

"A supply runner who doesn't know how long a run will take her?" He eyed me, and I got the feeling he might be shrewder than I'd given him credit for. "What are you really, Alana?"

I smiled at him. "Just another lowly human working for the empire to stay alive."

He looked like he didn't believe me, but I was telling the truth again. I'd been working for the empire to stay alive since they'd taken me when I was a child. I hadn't been given a choice when I'd been thrown into their academy and trained relentlessly. Now, I was the most lethal person in the Zagrath Empire, but I still worked for them. There was no other option in a galaxy where the imperial reach was long and their vengeance deadly. I should know. I was usually the one meting it out.

Tannel pressed his lips together and nodded. "If you do manage to stay alive, I'll be here."

Even though the Rellarian wasn't more than a bit of fun for me, I locked eyes with him. "You're a good guy, Tannel. You deserve someone who can give you a future. That isn't me."

He opened his mouth to argue, but I put my hand over his lips. "I can never give you what you want. Please believe me."

I turned sharply and strode up the ramp of my ship, not looking behind me. No matter what happened with the Vandar mission, I would not return to Rellaren.

"That's a fucking shame." I stomped through the ship, passing the last few imperial soldiers. I would miss the *menashi* and Tannel, but getting attached to either was a bad idea, and the Rellarian was clearly getting too close for comfort.

I huffed out a breath. Tannel wasn't the first male I'd left behind with a bruised heart, and he wouldn't be the last. My trail of abandoned lovers was almost as impressive as my trail of dead bodies.

"That's the last of it," one of the helmeted soldiers said as I headed to the cockpit. "You're all set."

"Good." The sooner I could take off the better. I had my orders, and I knew my mission. The imperial general had given me strict instructions. I was to pose as a female escapee from an imperial mining colony, and let my ship wander into Vandar space. Then I was to beg for assistance and be taken onto a Vandar horde. Since they were raiders, they would confiscate my cargo, which would allow the empire to track both it and me. When the Zagrath tracked down the horde, they would attack, and I would assassinate the warlord of the Vandar horde.

It wasn't foolproof—nothing was—but we knew that the Vandar monitored their space for encroaching ships. We also knew that the raiders had recently taken human females as part of their hordes. I knew the empire was using me for my looks as well as for my skills as an assassin. It was expected that I would use all my skills to make the Raas trust me, even if that meant seducing the brute and letting him claim me.

The thought of using my body didn't bother me. Sex had always been part of my arsenal. I'd learned early that males could be easily swayed by their cocks. The Vandar Raas would be no different.

I entered the compact bridge and saw the imperial soldier waiting for me. I'd almost forgotten this part of the plan.

"You are ready?" he asked drawing back his hand.

I fisted my hands, both pissed I hadn't gotten my *menashi* after all, and to brace myself for the blow. "Let's do this."

CHAPTER TWO

Bron

My *majak* leaned back on the bench and took a swig from his goblet of Vandar wine. "The Raas quarters suit you."

I took a gulp of wine, letting the sharp tang fill my mouth and burn its way down my throat. I placed my goblet on the shiny, ebony table that seemed too long and imposing for only two warriors. Then again, everything about the spacious suite felt like too much compared to the officer's quarters I'd previously occupied.

Peering out the wall of glass that overlooked the inky blackness of space, I blew out a heavy breath. "I keep expecting to see Kratos."

It had been many rotations since Raas Kratos had given up his horde in favor of staying on the Vandar colony of Zendaren with his human bride, who was expecting the first Vandar-human baby. Even so, it felt surreal that Kratos had appointed me to succeed him as Raas, and I was now occupying the Raas quarters that had once been his. I had spent much time in these quarters conferring with Kratos, but never had I expected to be residing in them myself.

My eyes scanned the large space with gleaming floors and walls as black as the eternal night beyond the glass. Chunky, dark furnishings were sparsely arranged and bolted to the floor so they would not slide during battle. The fire inset in one of the walls crackled with blue flames, producing dancing shadows in the dimly lit room, but not much heat. Not that I minded. Vandar needed little clothing, and we were never cold. Even the large bed, with its imposing headboard fashioned from iron battle axes welded together, was only covered in silky sheets the color of blood—a change from the black ones Kratos had used, and one of the few alterations I'd made to the Raas quarters.

"Of course, he is missed." Svar rested his thick forearms on the table. "But you have filled his boots admirably, Raas."

"I have yet to be tested." I flicked my gaze at the warrior who'd served with me on the command deck, and whom I'd elevated to the position of my first officer. "Neither of us have."

Svar met my eyes and nodded, obviously not taking my statement as a rebuke. "Because the Vandar have struck important blows to the empire, and our horde was part of that."

He lifted his goblet to me in toast. I joined him, clinking my glass with his and chugging the last of my wine. Instead of warming my belly, the pungent wine tasted sour as it twisted in my gut.

What he said was true, but it did not make me feel better. Along with two other Vandar hordes, we had destroyed an entire imperial fleet and prevented them from reaching our secret colonies and kept the Zagrath admiral from communicating his knowledge of our hidden people to the rest of the empire. As far as we knew, the Zagrath empire was back to square one in their hunt for our colonies and in their attempts to weaken us.

But all this had taken place before I'd taken over as Raas. Since I had been given control of the horde, things had been unnaturally quiet. We'd been patrolling our assigned sector with almost no incursions, and the Zagrath appeared to be in retreat, which was a victory for everyone in the galaxy who opposed imperial rule. Despite our apparent win, I could not allow myself to celebrate too much. Since I'd taken on my role as Raas, I had been unable to shake the sense of foreboding that dogged my thoughts and chased away my sleep.

"Until the empire is destroyed, our mission is unchanged," I said, my voice a throaty rumble.

Svar nodded. "But perhaps it is less difficult."

I shrugged. I'd chosen my *majak* because he had the ability to see victory in defeat. That, and I trusted him to be honest with me. Even still, I had not told him the nagging sense of doom I'd felt since our horde had lifted off the surface of Zendaren, and I'd officially been the warlord of my own horde. Admitting this would be admitting weakness, and I had watched Raas Kratos and his father Raas Bardon before him enough to know that weakness was a luxury a Raas could ill afford. Of course, I had not had a father to teach me like Kratos had. Was that why I felt tendrils of unworthiness snaking through my mind? Did I fear that my humble origins as an orphan made me weak?

I did not *feel* weak, but I did feel an uncontrollable frustration with my new role. Being called Raas did not fill me with pride like it should have, and that stoked a burning fury deep within me—one I fought to control.

"Tell me, *majak*." I steadied my temper and my voice as I reached for a brown knot of bread remaining on my plate. "Are the raiders getting restless? We have not engaged in battle since we left Zendaren."

Svar took another drink and shifted on the long bench, his tail swishing behind him like it did when he advised me. "It has been unusually quiet. Vandar are not used to peace."

I tore at the knot of bread with my teeth. "We could always find an imperial outpost to raid, although we do not need the supplies."

Svar braced his elbows on the table and threaded his fingers together, tilting his head at me. "The warriors would prefer a stop at a pleasure planet."

My thoughts wandered to the last stop at a pleasure planet and the time I'd spent with a pair of alluring Felaris twins, and I bit back a growl. If I closed my eyes, I could almost imagine the softness of their lips on mine and the warmth of four hands stroking my bare flesh. Then I remembered what had happened shortly after the twins had removed my battle kilt, and how quickly I'd been forced to throw it on again and race out of the pleasure house to defend our ship from mercenaries. "Our last visit was hurried."

"Most of the crew had barely chosen their pleasurer before we were returning to the ship," Svar said. "Including me, and I'd picked a particularly appealing Haralli."

"You always did like your females with wings."

He raised his palms. "What's not to like?"

When we'd last been on Jaldon, I'd been *majak* and not Raas. I'd been crucial to the command crew, but I had not been the Vandar who dictated the actions of the horde. I had not had the lives of so many in my hands.

I shook my head. "It is too soon after our time on Zendaren to make a stop at a pleasure planet." I swung my legs over the bench and stood. "The Zagrath may be weakened, but they need to feel our presence."

"Which lends strength to your argument that we should commence raiding."

I took long steps toward the fireplace, adjusting my shoulder armor as I walked. I was unused to the additional leather covering that further signified me as Raas, and it chafed at me in more ways than one. "Are the defenses on Carlogia holding?"

"The transmissions from Raas Kaalek indicate they are."

Our horde had joined forces with another to beat back Zagrath forces, and restore independence to the planet. It had been a violent battle, and the victory had been sweet. Even thinking about it made my pulse quicken.

I leaned one palm against the hard, obsidian stone and stared into the fire, trying to temper my desire for battle. "We should remain in our sector. Kaalek and Kratos might have repaired their relationship, but that does not mean Raas Kaalek wants his older brother's horde in his territory."

"It is not his brother's horde anymore, Raas," Svar reminded me. "You are Raas Bron, leader of this horde."

Tvek, I cursed to myself and curled my hand into a fist against the cool black surface. Why was it so hard to think of myself as Raas? Why did the mantle of warlord feel so oppressive on my shoulders?

Probably because the title of Raas of the Vandar had been handed down from fathers to sons or brother to brother for generations. I had been Kratos' *majak* and closest confidante, but we were not related by blood. His only blood relation on the warbird was Corvak, the battle chief, and Kratos had made it clear to me he did not believe his cousin was the best leader for his horde.

"You are sure, Raas?" I had asked when we'd stood on the balcony overlooking the feasting hall on Zendaren the night before the horde was scheduled to depart.

Kratos had clapped a thick hand on my shoulder. "I have never been more sure about anything." His mouth had quirked into a smile. "Aside from my mate."

"The horde has been in your family for generations," I'd reminded him. "What would your father say?"

Kratos had flinched at the mention of the Vandar Raas who had terrorized both of us when we'd been apprentices on his warbird. "Luckily for both of us, Raas Bardon is dead. The best thing for the horde is you."

I gazed now at the cavorting flames in my new quarters and hoped that Kratos had been right. As a Vandar raider who had led warriors into bloody battles, doubt was not a sensation I knew well or welcomed.

If Corvak had felt slighted by being passed over for the position of Raas, he had not indicated it. He had also not expressed displeasure when I'd chosen Svar as my *majak* instead of him. He remained as battle chief to the horde—a job he excelled in and seemed to relish. If he'd been removed as battle chief, he would have also been forced to give up his *oblek*, and his torture chamber was his sanctuary.

"How are you getting along with Corvak?" I asked as I turned from the fire to face Svar.

"Fine, Raas. We each know our positions and do our jobs." He spun around on the bench and splayed his hands on his knees. "I would say that he hungers for battle more than most."

I laughed darkly. "Then you do understand Corvak."

"If only there was someone to send to his *oblek*. That might quench his thirst for battle."

I dragged a hand through my long hair and thought about the room attached to one side of the command deck with weapons strapped to the walls and restraining chains dangling from overhead. "I would not wish many to Corvak's *oblek*."

"Nor I, unless they were Zagrath."

A pounding on my door made us both turn toward the steel arch. I strode to it and pressed the panel to one side, causing the two sides to part and reveal my battle chief.

"Just the Vandar we were talking about," I said, as I waved him inside.

He raised a dark eyebrow as he stepped inside, the scar on one side of his face making him look even fiercer than he was. "Oh?"

"We were saying that your *oblek* has been sadly underused" Svar stood and walked to join us at the door, the leather of his kilt slapping against his thighs.

Corvak nodded and he placed a hand on the carved hilt of his battle axe, his tail twitching behind him. "I cannot argue with you, but the news I bring may change that."

I exchanged a look with Svar as my heart thumped in my chest. "There is news?"

My battle chief gave a half shrug. "Not an imperial fleet, or even a Zagrath ship, but we have been tracking an unmarked freighter."

My attention pricked. "Unmarked? It is not imperial?"

"Not that we can tell." Corvak frowned. "And it is damaged."

"Life signs?"

"The freighter's hull appears to contain something that is muddling them."

My pulse quickened. That could indicate an imperial trap.

My *majak* huffed out a breath. "It is a sad day when a Vandar horde considers a damaged, unmarked freighter to be of interest."

Corvak slid a cold glance at Svar. "We have boarded freighters before and found them to be carrying imperial cargo."

I grunted. We all knew that the last time we'd boarded a freighter, our Raas had ended up taking one of the human females onboard as his captive. The battle chief had strongly opposed the move, and had never warmed to the small creature. "I am not sure the cargo was worth the trouble."

Corvak choked back a rough laugh. "I might be willing to agree with you, Raas, but a raiding mission is still a mission."

"Especially one that might be an imperial trap. Besides, I have no intention of taking prisoners," I added. Although I liked the human that Raas Kratos had eventually taken as his mate, her presence had been a disturbance on our warbird, and she was the reason Kratos was gone and I was now Raas. As much as I honored Raas Kratos, I had no desire to repeat his actions.

"Unless they are meant for my *oblek*?" Corvak asked.

I gave him a sharp nod, a sense of purpose swelling in my chest. What I needed to banish my doubt was blood dripping from my blade and battle cries filling my ears. I squared my shoulders. "*Vaes!* Tell the crew that their Raas has declared today to be a good day to die."

CHAPTER THREE

Bron

The steel floors rattled as I made my way through the warbird, Svar and Corvak flanking me as we descended to the hangar bay. Red lights flashed around us, reflecting off the exposed piping and suspended, iron walkways that created the labyrinth of the Vandar ship. Bare-chested warriors leapt from winding staircases to fall in step with us, their echoing footfall joining ours to create a drumbeat as we marched.

Corvak had sent out the battle call, and the command deck crew had immobilized the damaged freighter. Our horde remained unseen by our prey, thanks to our invisibility shielding. All the ship would know is that they could no longer move. They wouldn't understand that it was a Vandar attack until our raiding ships locked onto their hull. This was why many throughout the galaxy considered us wraiths—ghost ships who appeared out of nothing and portended death.

A warrior inside the hangar bay snapped his heels together as I passed through the broad, double doors. "Raiding ships ready for departure, Raas."

I inclined my head to him, surveying the black, birdlike ships lined up on the expansive, open floor. Curved wings stretched out from round bellies that were waiting to be filled with raiders, metal ramps extending to the floor like tongues. A wide mouth at the far end of the hangar bay opened up onto space, and an energy field hummed across it, keeping everything inside from being sucked out.

Pausing at the bottom of one of the ramps, I spun and raised a fist into the air. "All glory to Lokken, god of old!"

The raiders thrust their fists in the air. "Glory to Lokken!"

I thought of Kratos, and the many times he'd led us into battle with the familiar chants. I pumped my fist higher. "For Vandar!"

"For Vandar!" my crew bellowed in reply.

Even without Kratos leading the charge, the war cry both centered me and fired my blood. Our people had been using it since the days we'd roamed the open plains of our home world. It had been the Zagrath who had subjugated us and forced us to take to space, but we held tight to our traditions. Even though our galloping beasts had been replaced by iron ships, we still traveled in hordes of warbirds, and wore traditional battle kilts with long-handled axes swinging from our belts. Despite our advancements in technology, our beliefs in the old ways remained strong. Valiant warriors would live forever in Zedna with the gods of old, and it was our mission to rid the galaxy of imperial control and one day return our people to the home world of Vandar.

I pounded up the ramp, and my warriors followed close at my heels. Our bodies were pressed tightly together as we clutched steel beams overhead and the ramp slammed shut, then the engine rumbled beneath our feet and the ship thundered across the hangar bay floor and burst into space.

As I stood near the open cockpit, I had a clear view of the freighter as we approached. Battered and dented, it did not appear to be a warship of any kind. A powerful memory resurfaced. The ship we'd raided when Kratos had taken the human captive had looked similar to this—like a wounded beast not fit for anything but being put out of its misery.

"Why do I feel like I have been here before?" Corvak growled, shifting restlessly beside me.

I swallowed the hard knot of disappointment in my throat, remembering that a battle was still a battle. This ship might still be an imperial trap, I reminded myself. I gripped the hilt of my axe and prayed to the gods of old that there would be imperial blood to spill.

Our ship clamped onto the freighter with a hard jolt, the docking pincers holding us to the hull as lasers cut through the metal. When the hull was breached and our ramp slammed down, my raiders poured out and assumed our defensive formation.

I ran out with Corvak and Svar on each side of me. "We'll take the lead. The rest of you fan out and look for any signs of a crew." I glanced up. "Do not neglect to search the ventilation ducts and ceiling panels."

This ship was not as dated and rundown as the human ship I'd boarded with Kratos. Despite evidence it had been recently attacked—patches and scorch marks on the hull—the interior was in decent repair. The ambient lighting in the narrow corridors was low, illuminating the pale gray walls with a blue glow, and the only sounds came from our footsteps and the occasional computerized beep as we made our way toward the front of the ship.

Even though Corvak had informed me that our scanners hadn't been able to detect much in the way of life signs, he'd also admitted the scanners had been blocked. I'd held out hope that this meant an imperial fleet would be lying in wait for us, but there was no sign of that, or even a skeleton crew. What kind of freighter flew with no crew? It wasn't small enough to be a single-man ship, unless the captain was as bold as he was foolish.

Raiders peeled off in pairs as we continued through the corridors until Svar stopped and raised a fist. His eyes were locked on the scanner in his hand, and he jerked his head toward the sealed door in front of us. "I'm picking up a life sign, Raas."

"A life sign?"

He grimaced. "Just one."

So, the freighter contained a solo captain. I was irritated that all our effort had been for one person, but I was also intrigued. It was unthinkable for a Vandar to fly solo. We lived and fought together, and there was no concept of glory independent of our hordes. The only solo captains I'd met were battle-hardened aliens who came from species that valued living alone, or criminals who were on the run. I lifted my battle axe across my chest, curious what species of creature was on the other side of the door. "Let's meet this captain."

Corvak wedged the tip of his curved axe between the seam in the doors and forced it open with a roar, then he and Svar rushed inside. I followed with a loud battle cry, prepared to dodge blaster fire. But there was none.

Instead, my *majak* and battle chief stood on the compact command deck with their axes raised and their mouths open. The captain of the ship was not a brazen soldier, or even a grizzled smuggler. She was a female. A human female.

But she was not like the female captain who'd greeted Kratos with fury and defiance when we'd taken that ship. No, this creature sat slumped in the captain's chair with bruises on her face and blood trickling from a cut on her forehead.

Raising her head, she met my eyes with her own dark, slightly winged ones. "I knew someone would come to save me."

Save her? Corvak and Svar both swung their heads to me.

Tvek. I dropped my axe and groaned. We hadn't found a worthy opponent or a valiant battle. We'd found someone looking for rescue.

CHAPTER FOUR

Alana

"Took you long enough," I muttered under my breath as voices rumbled outside the door to the bridge.

Not only had I been floating in space with my engines powered down since second watch, but it had also taken the Vandar longer than I'd expected to reach me. My heart knocked against my ribs as the door was wrenched open, but it was from excitement, not fear.

It was finally time.

When they thundered onto the bridge, I kept my brow furrowed and my shoulders slumped to feign weakness. I didn't have to fake my injuries, though. When I was done with this mission, I was going to find the imperial soldier who'd been tasked with roughing me up and give him a little payback. He'd seemed to enjoy slapping me around a bit too much, and his blows had been harder than they'd needed to be to produce a nominal amount of bruising. As it was, my left cheek throbbed, and I was pretty sure one of my back teeth was loose. It would explain the metallic taste every time I swallowed.

I waited a beat until I lifted my head. "I knew someone would come to save me."

There were three raiders standing shoulder to shoulder in front of me. All were enormous with dark hair spilling over their shoulders. They wore leather kilts and lace-up boots, but little else. Their broad chests were bare except for the black swirling marks across their muscles.

Correction. One of them was not fully bare chested. He had buff-colored shoulder armor that buckled across his chest, and finely tooled leather sheathing his forearms. I assumed he was the one in charge, so I focused my attention on him.

He groaned and lowered his circular battle axe.

"It's another human, Raas," one of his fellow raiders said in the universal language.

Raas. The Vandar word for warlord—the leaders of their hordes. I'd never actually seen a Vandar Raas before, and I took a moment to take him in. The warlord's long hair matched the dark scruff covering his cheeks and framing full lips that were currently curved down in a scowl. A beige tail with a black, furry tip flicked behind him in obvious agitation, making him look every bit the predator. If I wasn't so deadly myself, I would have been terrified.

"I can see it is a human." The Vandar leader narrowed his eyes at me. "Who are you, and what are you doing alone in this sector, female?"

"Alana." I made my voice tremble as I spoke, reminding myself that most human women would be petrified to be facing three violent Vandar raiders. "My name is Alana."

"And this is a Raas of the Vandar," one of the other raiders said sharply. "You will address him as Raas, or Raas Bron and you will stand when you do so."

My gaze returned to the warrior whose dark eyes had never left me. So, this was Raas Bron. If I hadn't been in the middle of playing a damsel in distress, I would have cheered. Part of my mission was to find and kill Raas Bron, and here he was, in the flesh. I'd managed to lure the correct Vandar horde straight to me. I stood, making sure to appear unsteady on my feet and to hide my elation.

The Raas cocked an eyebrow and remained silent, clearly waiting for me to answer the rest of his questions.

"I wasn't alone, Raas," I said. "Not when I escaped from the Zagrath camp."

One of the other Vandar shifted from one foot to the other and cut his eyes to the leader.

"I was on Rularen III," I continued. "It's occupied by the empire."

The Vandar in charge hooked his axe on his waist and folded his arms across his chest. "Yes, we know. It's been converted into a mining colony."

I'd never actually set foot on Rularen III, but I'd studied enough about it. "That's right. We mined for rare minerals, although the mines have been running dry as of late. That meant angry imperial commanders. Some of us decided we were sick of taking Zagrath punishment, so we stole a ship and escaped."

The Vandar with a scar slashing his cheek spun the handle of his axe in one hand. "Where are the others now?"

I heaved in a breath and blinked quickly to manufacture tears. "Dead. The empire attacked as we escaped, and our ship suffered damage. Everyone else was either killed or wounded badly enough that they didn't survive."

"And their bodies?" he asked.

"I couldn't keep them in here." I looked down, willing tears to fall. "I put them out the airlock."

Footsteps rumbled from the corridor and more Vandar raiders entered the bridge, stopping and staring at me. Even though their arrival was unexpected, at least it took the Raas' attention from me for a moment, which was fortunate since I could *not* seem to be able to force out a tear. I burrowed my fingernails into the flesh of my palm, cursing myself for failing to manufacture sorrow—again.

Raas Bron did not turn his body, but he twisted his head slightly to address his raiders. "What have you found?"

"Very little food, Raas," one of the raiders answered after tapping his heels together. "And the ship is out of fuel."

"Signs of battle?" the other Vandar flanking the Raas asked.

A raider from the back of the group cleared his throat. "Hull breaches that have been sealed poorly."

"Mining supplies in the cargo bay, Raas," said another.

Raas Bron snapped his head back to me. "Maybe you are not lying."

I widened my eyes and pretended to be shocked. "Why would I lie?"

The scarred raider emitted a low growl.

"Raas," I added, quickly. I didn't know who the scarred guy was, but I was going to kill him as soon as I'd dispatched the Vandar warlord.

Both raiders flanking the Raas turned to him and began speaking Vandar in low voices. My pulse quickened. None of them sounded pleased, and I wasn't sure if they believed me or not.

The Zagrath general had assured me that the Vandar raiders were ruthless brutes who would be easy to trick and then seduce. He'd made them sound like violent aliens who cared about little but killing and fucking. As I watched them confer, I got my first inkling that this wasn't entirely true.

The leader turned back to me. "Consider yourself lucky, female."

I smiled at him, although even that slight movement made my face ache. "You're going to help me?"

"No." He spun on his heel and the leather flaps of his kilt caught air. "We are going to let you live." He motioned his raiders to the door. "*Vaes!*"

Fuck. Maybe I was wrong about them not being ruthless brutes.

"You're going to leave me without food or fuel?" I grabbed his arm before he stepped out of my reach. "You can't do that. You have to take me with you."

Axes were drawn so quickly even I was startled as multiple blades pointed at me, one coming so close to my face that a wisp of my dark hair was sliced off and fluttered to the floor.

Raas Bron held up a hand before any of his raiders could touch me. He bent low so that his words buzzed my ear. "You are wrong, human. I can do that. I am a Raas of the Vandar." He straightened and locked eyes with me, his dark and deadly. "I obey no one, especially not a female."

Heat arrowed through me, but I brushed it off and tried to ignore the blush threatening my cheeks. My mission was going off the rails fast. I had to get myself onto his horde, along with my cargo.

"You would leave me to die?"

His hand closed over mine, surprising me with its warmth, and he uncurled my fingers from his arm. "I would leave you for someone else to find. The Vandar do not rescue."

I rubbed the skin on my hand, my flesh hot from his touch. "Even someone who defied the Zagrath?"

The raiders shifted, and an uncomfortable murmur rippled through them. Most of the galaxy knew them as terrorists. The Zagrath had worked hard to solidify that reputation for them. But I knew they were a people pledged to fight against the empire and lend aid to planets who resisted imperial rule. I knew that because it was part of my job to ensure that their mission failed.

I tipped my head back. If playing the victim of the Zagrath wouldn't work, I'd have to shift to Plan B. I bit my bottom lip and leaned closer to him, making my voice a purr. "Please, Raas."

Raas Bron looked down at me. "There is no room for a female on a Vandar warbird."

So much for my feminine charms. I really was going to kill the imperial soldier who'd knocked me around. It was hard to be seductive when you could barely smile, and your lip was purple and swollen. My frustration was quickly morphing into rage, my pulse racing from fury, not fear.

I assessed the number of raiders and their weapons. Maybe I could take out the Raas right here. I wouldn't survive the fight, but at least I'd accomplish part of my mission.

No, Alana. The mission is to lead the empire to the horde. Assassinating Raas Bron is not enough.

"You can't even give me safe passage?" I begged. "I promise I won't be any trouble. You won't even notice I'm on your ship."

He scowled down at me then hissed out a breath. "I doubt that very much, human." Then he cut his eyes to one of the raiders beside him. "Bring her with us."

He stomped toward the door, leaving me with my mouth hanging open. It had worked? He was actually taking me on board his horde ship?

"Yes, Raas." The scarred Vandar clamped a hand over my bicep. "What about the rest of the ship?"

Raas Bron's tail flicked behind him, but he didn't turn. "We take nothing but the female. The rest we blow up."

My gut tightened. Blow up? The Zagrath general had also assured me that the Vandar would take the cargo and anything not bolted to the floor. They were raiders, after all, and were known for stripping ships bare.

I stumbled forward as the Vandar moved as one off the bridge, pulling me with them and following the Raas. If they didn't take the tracked cargo, the empire wouldn't be able to pinpoint the horde. They wouldn't be able to come for me. I considered asking if I could pack a bag, but decided that would be pushing my luck.

Leveling my gaze at the broad back of Raas Bron, I shook off my growing sense of panic. I'd had setbacks on missions before. It was nothing I couldn't overcome.

I was still the most deadly assassin in the empire. I *would* kill the Raas and destroy his horde. I swallowed again, this time welcoming the tang of the blood from my bloodied lip. I never failed.

CHAPTER FIVE

Bron

"Well?" I stood on my command deck and rocked back on the heels of my boots.

Corvak gave me a curt nod as the steel doors swished closed behind him. "It is done." He stared straight ahead as he joined me in looking over the warriors at their standing consoles. "You are sure we should not keep her in my *oblek?*"

I flicked my gaze to the doors leading to his special chamber. "You think we should hang an injured female from your chains?"

"What do we know of her, Raas? How can we be certain she is who she claims to be?"

I did not always see eye to eye with my battle chief, but he was correct about this. I knew little of the female who called herself Alana. Her bruises were real, and her ship's records had backed up her story, but that did not mean she could be trusted.

"She is in one of the officers' quarters," I said. "Not my chambers."

Corvak inclined his head, acknowledging that this was different than what our former Raas had done when he'd taken the human female as part of the spoils from a freighter we'd raided.

"But not guarded," he said.

Svar joined us, taking his post on my other side. "A female that slight is no threat to any Vandar on this ship."

I was inclined to agree with my *majak*, although I did not want to admit how carefully I'd studied the female's lithe body. It was true she was not tall, but it had not escaped my attention that her arms were roped with muscle, and the waist she attempted to hide under a baggy shirt was taut.

If she had been a worker on the imperial mining colony, it would make sense that she would be fit. The Zagrath were known for being relentless taskmasters. Still, I suspected she was not as weak and helpless as she appeared. Not if she'd managed to evade the Zagrath. I'd sensed a strength in her. Plus, she'd been brave enough to challenge a Raas of the Vandar. My encounter with her had stirred my blood like nothing else since I'd taken control of the horde.

Corvak shot a look across me at Svar. "No enemy should be underestimated."

"You are both correct," I said to settle the argument I sensed brewing. "She is no threat to our trained and deadly raiders, but she should not be underestimated." I turned to my battle chief. "Assign a raider to watch her, but do not guard her door."

Corvak raised an eyebrow. "He should not stop her from leaving her quarters?"

"I would like to test her," I said. "See what she does if she thinks she has free rein to move throughout the ship."

"Clever strategy, Raas." Svar chuckled. "Allow her to reveal her true intentions without using force."

Corvak growled, his top lip curling. "I still say I would get faster results if I were allowed to take her to my *oblek*."

I clapped a hand on the warrior's broad shoulder. "Let us try this, first."

"As you wish, Raas." Corvak snapped his heels together then spun toward the door. "It is done."

When he'd departed the command deck to carry out my orders, I faced Svar. "I might not want her under lock and key, but I also do not want her lingering as our guest any longer than necessary."

"We are not a transport ship," he said with a solemn nod.

"No, we are not. We are raiders." And the female had provoked feelings in me I could not indulge. I scowled as I pivoted back to face the wide view screen dotted with distant pinpoints of light. "Not that we have had anything to raid lately."

"You could not have known the female's freighter would be worthless, Raas." My *majak* cleared his throat. "Why did we not take the cargo, though?"

"After learning what the Zagrath did to Raas Kaalek, I do not trust any cargo they might have touched."

"You think it might have been used to track us?"

I shrugged. "If it was, we have eliminated that possibility by blowing it up." Watching the freighter ignite in a white-hot explosion had been the only satisfying part of the failed raiding mission—aside from the human's defiance. "And what did we need with mining supplies?"

"So, what are your orders regarding our guest and her imminent departure?" Svar asked.

I clasped my hands behind my back. The female might intrigue me, but it was dangerous to let myself be captivated by her. I needed her off the ship as quickly as possible. "What is the closest inhabited planet that is not controlled by the empire?"

My *majak* crossed to his post, sweeping his fingers across the dark console. After a few moments, he swiped one hand up and a star chart appeared on the view screen. One point of light blinked blue. "Ladvok Prime. Class-M planet with an industrial civilization that trades freely with other planets and has maintained self-rule."

"Anything of interest about the natives?" I asked, peering at the dot indicating the planet. "I don't think we've ever encountered them."

Svar tilted his head as he studied his console. "Nothing of concern. Bipedal, hairless creatures who wear elaborate outfits and headdresses. They're governed by elected regional leaders, and have a monotheistic religion that dictates most of their moral structure. Aside from that, they're peaceful."

"Monotheism?" I shook my head. One god? How could one single deity explain the entirety of the universe, when it was clear that many ancient gods had forged stars and planets through a series of violent battles that gave form to the void? Although Lokken was the chief god, there were many gods of old that birthed the heavens with their mighty axes.

Svar shrugged. "I did not say they were sophisticated or technologically advanced, Raas."

"Then how have they staved off the empire?" And how did I know so little about this planet in my sector? Granted, my sector was immense, and when I'd been *majak* to Raas Kratos, we had gone where we were needed, which meant planets that were being occupied by the empire. We did not touch peaceful planets, unless they were pleasure ones.

"From what I can tell, they have no precious minerals in their core. They are an agrarian society. I doubt the empire has much use for their planet. Or their people." He gave me a small smile. "I forgot to mention that the Ladvokians are only a metron high."

So, these aliens would barely reach my waist? I almost grinned at the thought of the human female living among these small creatures in garish headdresses. Instead, I gave my head a shake. "Will the human be safe there?"

Svar looked up. "There is nothing in our database about them being xenophobic. Perhaps we can reach out diplomatically and offer them an incentive?"

I let out a sigh. Yes, the faster I could rid the ship of the human, the better. Something about her made my stomach clench and my pulse race. The last thing I needed as a new Raas was a human who distracted my mind from the mission. "Agreed. Set a course for Ladvok and send a communiqué through back channels, so they do not know that their newest resident will arrive by Vandar horde."

"It is done, Raas." Svar's fingers danced across the flat screen of his console as he carried out my orders. "We will arrive at Ladvok in two-point-four standard rotations."

I swiveled on my heel and headed for my strategy room. I needed to study my star chart and determine our moves after we dropped off the human. I also needed to determine why the thought of leaving the human female on the alien planet made the muscles in my stomach harden to iron.

CHAPTER SIX

Alana

I reached the wall of the compact room and turned sharply. I'd been pacing the length of it since arriving on the Vandar warbird and being escorted to the quarters.

"Now what?" I whispered to myself, casting a glance at the tray of uneaten food resting across foot of the bed. I had no concept of time inside the ship and no timepiece, but I knew I'd been there for at least a full rotation. At least, it felt like it.

I blew out an impatient breath. I'd managed to be taken by the raider horde and positively identify the warlord I was supposed to assassinate. That was good. But the cargo tagged with imperial trackers had been blown up, along with the ship I'd been in. Not so good.

I ran over my options in my head for the hundredth time. I could probably take out Raas Bron, but then I'd be stuck on an enemy warbird with no chance of rescue. I'd gone on tough missions before, but killing a Vandar warlord while on his ship without backup wasn't tough, it was suicidal. As much as I was devoted to being the empire's most successful assassin, I'd rather keep that title while remaining alive.

I thought of the other title they called me in furtive whispers. The Mantis would not be defeated so easily.

I reached the other wall and slapped my palm on the gunmetal-gray wall. It didn't budge, but pain shot up my arm. Shit. Was the wall made out of iron or cement?

This ship wasn't like any I'd ever been on. Instead of enclosed corridors and sleek paneling, the warbird made me think of a steel skeleton. Everything was exposed and open with heavy beams and piping, creating a web-like maze that stretched up into the ship's dimly-lit core. I'd tried not to gape as I was led through the net of suspended bridges and swirling staircases, but none of my briefings had prepared me for the reality of the dark and echoing ship and the hulking bare chested raiders who thundered through it in their leather kilts and glinting battle axes.

I glanced at the bed and the pale gray sheet tucked tightly around it. I guessed I should be grateful the mattress wasn't just a slab of metal. Sinking down onto it and pushing the food tray aside, I rested my elbows on my knees and attempted to calm my breathing.

"This is only a setback. You've had setbacks before. You can do this."

Somehow, the pep talk didn't help. I'd had setbacks before, but I'd never reacted to a target like I'd reacted to Raas Bron. I glanced at the top of my hand where his touch had scorched my skin. It was unblemished, but I could almost feel the heat when I thought of his skin brushing mine.

I shook my head. "Get it together, Alana. None of that matters. You have a job to do."

A job that included killing the huge warlord who'd made my pulse race and my mouth go dry. Memories of his dark eyes locked onto mine sent heat pulsing between my legs. I groaned and buried my head in my hands. So much for being the toughest, most cold-blooded assassin in the imperial fleet.

My mind drifted back to the Zagrath training camp. There had been no choice when I'd been in training. I had to be tough, or I'd end up dead. Only the strongest and most ruthless made it through the assassin training. It was why the Zagrath never sent their own kind through the program. They considered themselves too valuable to be wasted. But aliens that they plucked from occupied planets were another matter, especially if they were chosen as children.

I could barely remember my life before being taken by the Zagrath. My parents were a fuzzy memory, although their screams when I'd been ripped from them were not. I squeezed my eyes tight, trying to push the recollection back down into the dark recesses of my brain. If I didn't think about it, I wouldn't wonder what happened to them. If I didn't allow myself to consider the probable outcome of that encounter, they remained alive and well on Faaral.

I balled my hands into fists and pressed them into my closed eyes. It didn't matter now. None of that mattered. The only thing that mattered was the mission. The only thing that mattered was success. That had been drilled into me so thoroughly I was sure it was imprinted on my human DNA.

Success meant approval. Approval from the empire meant that I belonged. Even though I was not technically one of them, being their top assassin meant I was a valuable part of the empire. It meant I was important. I let the feeling of importance and belonging wash over me like a cascade of warm water, and my heart slowed to a steady beat.

"That's right," I told myself, snatching a hard knot of bread off the tray and biting into it. "The empire needs you. They can't succeed without you."

I swallowed the hard bread and sat up, squaring my shoulders and remembering every commendation I'd been given and every Zagrath leader who had looked at me with respect and a little bit of fear. To most of the empire, I was invisible, but *they* knew who I was. I was the key to their victories. I was the one who'd taken out chiefs and potentates and royalty, and paved the way for imperial forces to sweep in unopposed. I was the Mantis. A Vandar horde was nothing I couldn't handle.

Standing, I crossed to the reflective surface above a utilitarian dresser. I swept my fingers through my dark hair and leaned closer to examine my face. The bruises hadn't faded on my olive skin yet, and half of my face looked like a mottled patchwork of purple and blue. I appraised my own brown eyes, glad the imperial soldier hadn't blackened them. I should have snapped that guy's neck, I thought.

"As soon as I'm done here," I promised myself.

As it was, I'd need to rethink my strategy of seducing Raas Bron. Not only did I look pretty scary, but he also hadn't reacted to my flirtation at all. *I'd* been the one to practically go weak at the knees when he'd touched me, and that was *not* part of the plan.

If I couldn't seduce him, I'd have to figure out another way to take out the warlord and lead the empire to the horde. Everyone had a weakness. I'd just have to figure out his. I eyed my face again. Or get my hands on a serious amount of concealer.

I walked to the door and pressed my ear to the surface. Like everything on the ship, it was thick metal, and I couldn't hear a thing except for the muffled cacophony of raiders moving about the ship, heavy boots pounding against iron. I held my breath as I pressed my hands at the seam of the steel door and attempted to pull the two sides apart. When they didn't budge, I slammed my hand on the wall in frustration. The door slid open silently.

Peering more closely at the wall, I noticed that it was an inset panel. Clever. I looked back at the open door. They'd left it unlocked. I grinned. Not so clever.

I peeked outside the room. No massive raider stood guarding the door. They'd left me unattended, as well. Maybe I'd overestimated the Vandars' intelligence.

I smiled to myself, thinking that the Vandar might just be dumb brutes after all. Then I hesitated, as I remembered how shrewdly the Raas had studied me. Or perhaps he was even more clever than I'd expected. I bit the corner of my lip. Was I luring him into my web, or was he tricking me into falling into his?

CHAPTER SEVEN

Bron

Corvak entered my strategy room and opened his mouth the speak, then belatedly clicked his heels together.

"Report," I said, standing and coming around the large ebony desk.

"It is the female."

My pulse stirred as if I'd been stalking prey which had finally moved. "She's left her quarters?"

Corvak tilted his head. "No. Actually, she opened the door and looked outside, then went back inside and has not left the room since."

"That is unexpected."

"Agreed, Raas." My battle chief stroked a hand along the scar that ran down one cheek. "Unless she is what she said she is."

I turned and strode to the wall of glass that looked out onto space, leaning one hand on the cool surface. "A female stranded in space in need of rescue?"

"It has happened."

I twisted to look back at him. "Weren't you the one who was convinced that the female Kratos took was a danger? Did you not agree that we should watch this female?"

"I was right about Kratos' Raisa. She was the reason our ship was boarded and then attacked."

He had a point. "That was no fault of hers." When Corvak didn't respond, I continued. "Do you think taking this female poses a danger to our horde?"

He shifted from one foot to the other, resting one hand on the iron hilt of his axe. "This female does not have anyone to miss her or chase after her like the female Kratos took. At least, if her story is true. I do not know how much effort the empire will put into hunting down a single escaped miner."

"If that is what she is."

Corvak closed the gap between us and joined me at the floor-to-ceiling window. "I am unused to this, Bron."

I cut my eyes to him. Even though we were alone in my strategy room, it was not customary for any other raider to call me by my given name. Then again, he had addressed me as Bron for as long as we'd known each other.

"Me being Raas?" I asked.

He blinked at me, then shook his head. "That I am becoming used to. I am unaccustomed to you being the more suspicious one of us."

I choked back a laugh. "That *is* unusual."

"You did not suspect the last female we brought on board." Corvak eyed me. "Why this one?"

I could not tell him that I needed a reason to put distance between myself and the human. I wanted to discover some treachery or deception that would make it easy to drop her on Ladvok and never look back. Otherwise, I feared the desire that gnawed at my gut would consume me.

"I have not been Raas for long," I finally said. "I cannot afford mistakes."

Corvak nodded. "You also cannot afford to second-guess your commands. You are Raas."

I eyed him. I relied on my battle chief for shrewd war strategy, but had never turned to him for counsel. I was surprised by the wisdom of his words. Before I could tell him so, there was a thumping on the door.

"*Vaes*," I called out.

Svar stepped inside when the doors slid open, his gaze moving from me to Corvak and back again.

"Are we still on course to Ladvok?" I asked.

"Affirmative, Raas." He cleared his throat. "I come to convey a request."

I cocked an eyebrow. "From?"

"The female." He set his feet wide as he faced me, his hands clasped in front of him. "She wishes to bathe."

It took a few moments for the issue with the request to occur to me. The only bathing chambers available to raiders were communal ones with vast showers meant to be used by many at once. Not only that, but the controls for the water were also higher than a human could reach. Clearly, this would not work for the female.

I remembered the sad state of her clothing and her person when we'd found her. It was no wonder she wished to wash all traces of her ordeal from her flesh. My thoughts wandered to her flesh unencumbered by her dirty, loose garments, and desire skimmed across my own skin followed by a tremor of unease.

"Take her to my quarters," I spat out. "She can use the Raas bathing pools."

Silence hung in the air, and my two advisors glanced at each other.

Finally, Corvak spoke. "You wish the female to be taken to your quarters?"

"To bathe. Nothing else." I scowled and gave my head a hard shake. "I have told you before. I am not Kratos. I have no desire to keep this female for myself."

"It would be your right to take any female prisoner as the spoils of war," Svar said with a small shrug. "No one would judge you, Raas."

I studied my battle chief's stormy expression and doubted that was entirely true. The truth was I didn't know what I desired. I had not been Raas as long as Kratos had been when he had claimed his female. I could not afford such a dalliance. Still, the thought of depositing the human on an alien planet and never seeing her again made me want to hit something. "I am in no need of a mate or a Raisa, but that does not mean we cannot treat the human well while she is on our warbird. If she truly ran from the empire, then we are on the same side of justice."

"Of course, Raas." Svar tapped his heels. "I will have a raider escort her to your quarters. Do you wish her to be guarded?"

I gave Corvak a knowing look. "Not inside the chamber, but I would like to ensure she does not wander beyond it. In case we are not on the same side of justice after all."

Corvak tipped his head at me. "It is done."

"Send fresh food and wine to my quarters for her," I said. "She may still be hungry."

"Will you join her, Raas?" Svar asked.

I hesitated, thinking of seeing the dark-haired female across from me at the table. It would be enjoyable to share a meal with someone other than Svar and Corvak. Then I remembered the arousal that had fired my blood when I'd touched her.

No. If I had no thoughts of claiming her, I should not tempt myself with her company. I was already playing with fire by bringing her aboard and allowing her into my quarters. At least I would not be there to see her luxuriating in the bathing pools and sipping Vandar wine.

"I will not." I took long strides to pass both warriors, pausing at the door. "If you need anything, I will be testing out our new holographic battle ring. It has been too long since I've battled a *gorgomil*, and I look forward to seeing if the artificially created tentacles are as challenging as the real ones."

I didn't wait for their response as I left my strategy room and walked through the command deck, raiders at their consoles clicking their heels together at the sight of me. I made my way through the ship quickly, leaping from one open walkway to another. The dark interior of the warbird echoed my pounding footfall as I descended further into the ship's belly until I'd finally reached the newly installed holographic battle ring, a gift from Raas Toraan after the warlord brothers had reunited.

I tapped my fingers on the control panel, setting a program to battle the Jenvarian creature, and selecting the highest level of difficulty. I drew in a long breath as the door to the chamber opened, and I caught a glimpse of the enormous beast with flailing, spiked tentacles. My heart raced, but I didn't care. If I was battling a monster, at least my mind wouldn't be on the female I would soon be sending away. The one I secretly wanted for myself.

CHAPTER EIGHT

Alana

The raider led me into the spacious quarters and waved a hand in the direction of an arched doorway. "The bathing chamber is there."

I bit back a sarcastic retort, since it was pretty clear where the bathing pools were. The rest of the large room was sparsely furnished, with dark chairs and a long table flanked with benches secured to the floor, and there was only a single doorway leading into another space.

You're a scared female who escaped from the empire, I reminded myself. *Not a snarky assassin.*

"Thanks," I said, attempting to make my voice sound frail. "It will be nice to bathe."

The Vandar's gaze did not meet mine, but he nodded. "I will remain outside if you need anything."

"Outside the bathing chamber?" I asked, forgetting to soften the edge in my voice.

He glanced up at me, cocking one eyebrow.

Shit. That had sounded anything but unsure and fragile. I cleared my throat. "I mean, I doubt I'll need anything."

"And I meant that I will be outside the main door."

I let out a breath. "It's been a while since I had an actual bath. I might be in there a while." And I did not want anyone walking in on me while I searched the Raas' room.

"That is fine." He turned and headed for the exit. "When you are done, I will be waiting to escort you back to your quarters."

"Great." I managed to make that sound sincere, although it took effort. I also gave him a smile, but it was wasted on his retreating back. No matter. I kept it plastered on my face until the steel door closed, and I was alone. Then I spun around and scanned the room intently. "It's about fucking time."

Even though I'd told the guard I'd take a while, I did not want to get caught executing my imperial orders. I needed to work fast so I could hop in the bathing pools and make myself look like a woman who'd had a luxurious soak.

A cursory sweep with my gaze told me that a search wouldn't take long. There was barely anything in the room. No monitor or desk, or even a bedside table. To call the quarters spartan would have been an understatement, although the effect wasn't unpleasant.

A glossy, black table ran near the far wall with two long benches tucked on either side. The wall behind it was entirely glass and overlooked space—lights streaking past it a stark reminder that we were on a massive spaceship traveling close to warp speed.

The opposite wall held an inset fireplace in which blue flames gyrated like Orlenians engaged in a tribal dance. A pair of chairs were angled in front of the fire along with a low table—all the same high-polished ebony as the obsidian floors and ceiling. One of the only things *not* black was the enormous bed's imposing headboard, which had been forged from many battle axes, the steel glinting in the faint light from the flames. If I didn't already know that the Vandar were seriously violent, badass warriors, this room would have clued me in pretty quickly.

I strode to the bed, trying not to think about Raas Bron tangled up in the claret-colored sheets that were pulled tight across the surface. I reached one arm under the mattress, groping wildly. Nothing. So much for the Raas stashing something secret under there.

I stood and twisted around. I wasn't even sure what I expected to find, but most of my powerful and important victims had kept secret ledgers or devices or even journals in their private chambers. My mission wasn't just to take out Raas Bron. I needed to find the information that could take down the entire Vandar species.

Heading to the built-in dresser, I threw open the doors. A few leather kilts hung over a series of drawers. I quickly searched the contents of each drawer and found nothing but swaths of heavy fabric and wide belts.

"Come on, Bron," I whispered as I slammed the last drawer shut and closed the dresser doors. "You must have something personal in here."

Unless Vandar didn't keep personal items. I'd already seen that their ship was utilitarian to the extreme and their clothing minimalist. The only things that appeared to be individual were the carved handles or intricate etchings on the battle axes that swung by each raider's leg. Otherwise, their kilts and lace-up leather boots were standard issue. At least for ancient, nomadic warriors, which I knew their people had been.

Huffing out a breath, I took long steps across the room. I peered under the table and both benches then walked back across to the fireplace, daring to run my fingers along the inside rim of the hearth. It was surprisingly cool, but held no secret compartment.

"Fuckity fuck." I put my hands on my hips and darted a glance to the door. I needed to pick up my pace before I got busted hanging out in the Raas' quarters and not bathing. With another impatient sigh, I headed for the arched doorway leading into the adjoining chamber, pulling off my shoes as I alternated walking and hopping on one foot.

I stopped short when I entered the room. Now this was a surprise. Not that it looked dramatically different from the rest of the quarters—the black-stone decor theme was still going strong—but it held the most unusual bath I'd ever seen.

Shaped like a half-moon, the sunken tub was huge and divided into four wedges. Each of these wedges was filled with a different color of water. Steam rose from the crimson section, bubbles danced along the surface of the orange water, the green water was completely opaque, and the blue wedge of water was crystal clear.

I forgot my frustration as I peeled off the rest of my grimy clothes and left them on the floor. What I'd told the Vandar was true. It had been ages since I'd had a real bath, and I'd never had one in vividly hued water like this.

I padded barefoot to the edge of the pools. "Maybe Vandar aren't brutes about everything."

I dipped one toe in the steaming red water and almost moaned. It was hot, luxuriously and decadently hot. None of the imperial ships had water this hot, and the outposts that I'd been frequenting barely boasted tepid water—on a good day. I lowered myself into the pool, my skin stinging slightly from the heat but adapting quickly. When I'd sunk down so the water reached my chin, I closed my eyes.

It was hard to be too concerned with my mission when every muscle in my body was uncoiling. I inhaled deeply, a faint spicy aroma filling my nose and relaxing me even more. What had I been so stressed about? I'd barely arrived on the horde ship. I had plenty of time to take down the Vandar and kill Raas Bron.

I frowned as I thought about the fierce Vandar warlord. The gorgeous, fierce Raas. Why had I reacted to him the way I had? He was just a male, after all. I had plenty of experience with males of many species. Some quite enjoyable. But no male had made my pulse quiver and my mouth go dry before. Not even when they'd made me come. What kind of dark warrior was this Raas Bron to make me feel something so uncontrollable? My entire existence was about control.

I shook my head to rid myself of the conflicted feelings. The Vandar Raas was still my target, despite what he'd made me feel. And I still had to assassinate him. My stomach tightened, and I bit my lip, forcing myself to think of him dispassionately as just another mark, my mind racing with a risk assessment.

This one would not be easy to kill, especially since no raider seemed to go anywhere without their huge, deadly axe. And if the rumors were correct, they wielded their weapons with impressive skill. My mind whirred as I considered how to divest him of his axe. The axe was key.

"That's it!" My eyes flew open, and my heart fluttered with excitement. The Vandar battle axes. The only thing the Vandar personalized were their weapons, so maybe the battle axes that had been welded into a giant fan-like headboard held some sort of secret. "That's fucking it!"

I pulled myself out of the water and ran out of the bathing chamber, leaving a series of puddles in my wake. I didn't have time to dry myself or put my clothes back on. Not when I was sure I was onto something.

I leapt onto the bed and leaned close to the array of axes, squinting to inspect the etchings on the circular blades and the markings on the ornate handles. Most were ornamental or symbolic—swirls that mimicked the ones on their chests, or carved planets and stars—but it was the Vandar words I was most interested in. I'd taught myself basic Vandar before the mission, so I wasn't an expert, but I could read the words that appeared most often—Zedna, Lokken. These were words I recognized as part of the alien race's ancient mythology. I forced myself onto the tips of my toes as I peered higher to the largest axe at the center of the fanned design, and my breath hitched in my throat. I ran my finger over the one word that wasn't part of the mythology I'd learned about the Vandar—a word that was written over and over next to the image of a planet—*Zendaren*.

"Found you," I whispered, clenching my hand into a fist.

Then the door behind me opened and I froze, naked and dripping water onto the Raas' crimson sheets. *Fuck me.*

CHAPTER NINE

Bron

I stopped when I entered my quarters. I'd expected the female to be in the bathing pools when I entered to retrieve a fresh battle kilt. My plan had been to get a clean garment and discard the one currently stained with sweat from my bout with the holographic *gorgomil*. I'd be in and out before she'd notice, and I wouldn't come close to the door of the bathing chamber, or chance a glimpse of her naked. I had not intended to walk in on her completely bare and dripping water as she stood on my bed facing away from me.

The Vandar who'd been guarding the door inhaled sharply behind me, snapping me out of my stupor. I turned to the raider, whose mouth hung open unabashedly as he gaped at the human's lithe, naked body and her perfect, plump ass.

"I will handle this," I said, pressing the panel for the door to close on him before he could respond.

Alana's head swiveled around to look at me, her eyes closing briefly when she saw it was me. "I can explain, Raas."

I walked slowly toward the bed, even as my cock swelled beneath my kilt. "I would like to hear it."

She fisted her hands by her side as she pivoted to face me, her chin lifted slightly. If I'd thought she was appealing from behind, I was not prepared for the sight of her round breasts glistening with water, and the bare flesh of her sex. Her beige nipples were pebbled in the cool air, and I fought the urge to touch the bumpy skin that she made no attempt to cover.

I stopped at the foot of the bed, my gaze never leaving her. "I thought humans were known for their primitive modesty."

Her eyes flashed at me. "Not all humans."

Behind the flare of her pupils, I saw the flicker of pain, and a hint of the steely determination I'd detected on her ship. But was the pain from her life as a miner under imperial rule? I suspected there was more depth to her hurt, and that her strength came from more than a single escape.

She walked to the foot of the bed until she was close enough to touch, but I didn't move. Even though my body throbbed with the need to run my hands over her smooth skin, I kept my arms stiff and clasped in front of me in a vain attempt to hide my cock's traitorous response. As much as my mind knew that the human was the last thing I needed, my body did not seem to agree. Then again, never had a female presented herself so willingly who had not been a resident of a pleasure house.

"I am waiting for your explanation," I managed to say, even though my voice was thick.

Alana smiled down at me. My head was at the level of her stomach, and she stepped so close that I could feel the heat of her skin. She placed her hands on my shoulders. "Help me down, Raas?"

Tvek. I gritted my teeth as my cock strained painfully against my clasped hands. I might be a disciplined warrior, but I was still a hot-blooded male. The sound of my pounding heart filled my ears like a roar, and I had to close my eyes to steady my pulse and regain my control.

"Raas?" she purred, her fingers feathering across my shoulders.

Without opening my eyes, I clasped her by the waist and swung her down onto the floor. When her feet were on the hard stone, I peered down at her. The female's head was tipped up, and her brown eyes met mine, the lashes damp and dark.

I cleared my throat. "Do you think that your naked body will distract me enough that I forget my questions?"

Something flickered behind her eyes—anger? frustration?—but then she gave me a sultry smile. "What was your question, Raas? I'm afraid being so close to you has made me forget."

Her girlish voice and shy laugh should have convinced me of her distraction, but they only made me wonder about this female who was so clearly trying to convince me that she was harmless.

"What were you doing standing on my bed?" I asked, forcing my gaze not to wander below her face. "Wet and unclothed?"

She inclined her head slightly, as if conceding to me. "If you must know, I was curious about your headboard. I have never seen one like it."

I glanced behind her at the axes forged together to create a massive iron fan of blades, their edges still sharp enough to draw blood. Even though I knew that it had been created from the weapons of the earliest Raas' who had taken to the skies, I did not share this with the human. "Curious enough to inspect it while naked and dripping water from the bathing pools?"

She shrugged. "Everything on a Vandar ship is new to me. Does me being naked and wet bother you?"

My heart thudded in my chest as she licked her bottom lip. If she wished to play this game, then I could play, as well. My hands still spanned her waist, so I moved her back until her legs hit the bed, then I forced her to fall back. When she was lying on the bed, her knees bent and dangling over the side, I hovered over her and braced my elbows on either side of her body, pinning her arms to her. "It does not bother me. I thought you might be the one who wished to be clothed in the presence of a Vandar raider. Do I need to remind you that I am Raas of this horde? I can do anything I wish, and no one would dare stop me. You could scream until your throat was raw, and no Vandar would help you. On this ship, you are the property of the Raas, and I can do anything I wish with you."

She gazed up at me, blinking languidly. "I am not afraid of you, Raas, or wish I was clothed."

I used my knees to part her legs and settled my body between them. Her pupils widened and the pulse in her neck throbbed. "I do not think that is entirely true," I studied her face, "or entirely false."

Her breath was fast and shallow, her chest rising and her hard nipples brushing against my bare skin. I bit back a moan. This human was not like the one Kratos had taken. She was not sheltered and scared. Even though there was pain and fear behind her eyes, there was something more, something stronger. Something that gave me pause.

Before I could pull back from her, Alana jerked a hand free, raking her fingers through my hair and crushing my mouth to hers. My shock quickly gave way to blinding passion as our lips moved roughly and our tongues battled. Pressing my body to hers, I ground my cock between her legs as she moaned into my mouth.

Need stormed through me as all rational thought abandoned me, replaced by a haze of wanting. I ran one hand down the length of her body, tugging her leg up so it hooked around my waist and feeling the slickness between her thighs. It would take a mere flick to move aside the leather strips of my battle kilt and bury my cock inside her.

Take her. You are Raas.

The insistent words in my head made me falter. I was Raas, but I was not Kratos. I did not want a female to warm my bed, or distract me from building my own legacy. Not when I had barely begun. I reared up and dislodged her leg from my waist, staggering back and taking a shuddering breath.

Alana sat up, her eyes half-lidded and her legs slightly splayed. "What's wrong, Raas?"

"This," I said as I spun and took uneven steps to the door. "This can never happen again."

I jammed my hand against the panel to open the door and stumbled out, grateful when the door slid closed, even though the guard's expression was startled.

I straightened and raked a hand through my hair, my skin tingling from her touch. "Return the female to her quarters and make sure she remains there."

CHAPTER TEN

General Hardin stared at the imperial tactical officer who'd brought him the news. "What do you mean, the ship was destroyed?"

The officer kept his chin high and his eyes averted. "The trackers in the ship's cargo stopped transmitting, so we sent a ship to investigate. All that remains where the freighter last transmitted is debris from a major explosion."

Hardin leaned his hands against his desk, fighting the urge to scream. "We're sure it's *her* ship?"

"We've brought the debris back to analyze, General, but it appears to be the freighter she flew off Rellaren."

The general straightened and walked from behind his desk to the glass overlooking space. He ran a hand over his short hair, glad he could not see the gray hair that was overtaking his temples. "Any signs of the Mantis being part of the explosion?"

The officer cleared his throat behind him. "None that we have detected, General. It seems she was taken off the ship before it was destroyed." He hesitated. "Or she left."

Hardin flinched. "I suppose we have no indication of Vandar presence?"

"Once we search the debris, we might come up with some data on the ship's final moments, but so far we have no way to know who destroyed the freighter."

The general fisted his hands by his sides. "It was the Vandar. It had to be."

"I thought the Vandar were supposed to take the cargo, sir. I thought they were raiders who always stripped ships bare."

That detail bothered Hardin, as well. The Vandar should have taken the cargo. It was what they did, especially since the freighter was imperial. He shook his head to dismiss the concern. As long as they took Mantis, the plan was still in play.

"It doesn't matter." He spun around. "She will not fail. She's never failed."

The officer drew in a long breath before speaking. "It has already been several rotations, and we have heard nothing from her. How long do you wish to wait before we consider that she might have been unmasked as a spy and executed by the Vandar?"

Hardin bit back a retort. The officer was only doing his job—and he was right. They could not assume that the Vandar had fallen for the trap. After all, they'd blown up the freighter when all indications were that they would take the cargo instead.

"It has not been long enough to give her up as dead." He pivoted back to the view of space. "But our plan hinges on her alerting us to the horde and killing the Raas. If she has been rendered unable to do that…"

"We would be back to the beginning," the officer finished his sentence for him.

Hardin focused on a distant point of light, flickering brighter than the others. "Not if we send in someone to assist her."

"Assist her? I thought the Mantis only worked alone."

"She is part of the empire. She will do what is required." The general tore his gaze from the star and strode back to stand behind his desk. "If we have heard nothing from Mantis, either she has been killed, or she is unable to complete her mission." He did not mention the other possibility—that she had intentionally failed—because that was impossible.

"Should I alert the other operative that his skills will be required after all?"

General Hardin gave a single, sharp nod. "Send him in after her. It will be impossible for two assassins to fail." He leaned forward and braced his arms wide on his desk, giving his tactical officer a menacing grin. "I will have the Vandar warlord's head one way, or another."

When the officer left, he curled his hands into hard balls. And if Mantis had betrayed the empire, he would have her head as well.

CHAPTER ELEVEN

Alana

"I'm coming," I snapped, as the Vandar guard prodded me down the walkway. I tugged at the fabric clinging uncomfortably to my wet skin and let out a huff. I'd barely had time to throw on my clothes after the Raas had left and the guard had stormed in, ordering me to get dressed and come with him. There had been no time to towel off, even if I'd been able to locate a towel.

When we reached the quarters to which I'd been assigned, the guard opened the door for me and stood back for me to enter, not meeting my gaze. I stepped in, and the steel doors slid together, leaving me right back where I'd started—alone in the small room with no way to complete my mission.

I flopped onto the narrow bed. What had gone wrong? I'd had the Raas right where I'd wanted him—between my legs and delirious with desire. Then he'd stopped for no apparent reason, and run away like he'd been told I had a Pernithian bubble rash.

"You're losing your touch, Alana," I whispered to myself as I stared up at the gray ceiling. I'd never lost control of a male who'd been so close. And he had been close—that much I'd felt as it had pressed urgently between my thighs. So, what had happened? More importantly, why had I ached for his touch as his body had moved eagerly against mine?

I'd seduced more than my fair share of males and killed most of them. But this time, my moans in response to his touch had been real, as had been my disappointment when he'd staggered away from me. So, why did this one send sharp stabs of desire through me and make heat pool in my belly when none of the others had? The Mantis doesn't feel desire, I reminded myself, although my words were clearly a lie..

"It doesn't matter. He's still your mission, and you still have to kill him."

If he'd let me get near him again.

The Vandar were more complicated than I'd given them credit for. Especially Raas Bron. He hadn't been swayed by my seductive words, or even my sweet-girl-gone-naughty routine when he'd insisted I explain myself. Most males would have forgotten their question—and probably even their own name.

"Bron obviously isn't most males." I sat up and walked to the mirror, studying my face and the bruises. At least they were fading, although my task would be a lot easier if I didn't look like I'd gotten the worse end of a Tartillan cage match fight.

I clearly needed to reevaluate my strategy. I'd had the Raas in bed, and he'd still escaped my grasp. Now I was back in isolation, with little chance to seduce him or lead the Zagrath to the horde. Since the cargo had been destroyed, I was all but invisible to the empire. Not that they'd send a rescue party for me even if they knew where I was. That wasn't how my job worked. If I got caught or killed, the Zagrath would never claim me. As valuable as I was to them, my anonymity was even more important.

I smacked my palm against the wall, welcoming the sharp sting. I hated failing. It was an unfamiliar sensation and one that tasted bitter in my mouth.

"If I can't seduce Raas Bron, I need to focus on the other part of the mission," I said as I turned and paced a tight circle from one end of the small room to the other. I'd already obtained valuable intel. At least, I thought it was valuable. And drawing the empire to the Vandar horde and bringing about the destruction of their kind was the more important part of the mission anyway. Assassinating the Raas would be pointless if the horde remained intact.

I glanced at the steel door. Was the surly guard still on the other side? I know I hadn't been guarded earlier, but that was before I'd been caught naked on the Raas' bed.

"Only one way to find out," I muttered, as I took tentative steps toward the arched door. Pressing a hand to the side panel, I held my breath as the two sides of the door glided open.

That was a good sign. I wasn't locked in. I poked my head out and swiveled it from side to side. There was no sign of the unpleasant Vandar who'd marched me back to my quarters. I released a breath. More good news.

Stepping from the room, I hesitated. The Vandar warbird remained a mystery to me. I didn't know where I could find a communications center, or any place on the ship that would allow me to send a transmission or activate a beacon. For all I knew, there was no such place on board. It wasn't like the Vandar were known for communications. If anything, they moved throughout space without any hint of their existence.

I clenched my hands into fists. That didn't mean I wouldn't try. I couldn't spend the rest of my time on board waiting alone in a tiny room. I had to at least attempt to alert the empire and relay my intel.

"Then I'll figure out how to kill Raas Bron, if he won't be easily seduced."

Content with my new plan, I picked a direction and crept down the walkway. Above me, feet thudded loudly, and voices echoed as they bellowed through the shadows. For once, I was grateful for the aliens' bulk and ferocity. There was no way one of the huge raiders with thick boots and booming voices could sneak up on me.

Every time the metal floor beneath me rumbled, I ducked down a different corridor or pressed myself flat into a darkened doorway, content to let the dimness hide me. I cautiously opened door after door, but none of them revealed anything but spartan quarters that made the room I'd been assigned look almost opulent.

After a while, I wasn't sure if I'd be able to trace my way back to my assigned room. The maze of open-weave walkways seemed never ending and unchanging—each metal door and each spiraling staircase just like the dozen before it.

Was it possible to get lost in a Vandar warbird and never be found? I would have punched something if there was anything around me that wasn't iron and wouldn't have broken all the bones in my hand.

"Come on, Alana," I said under my breath. "You survived the swamps on Morrena. You can do this."

My mind flashed back to the toxic marshes on the alien planet, and the fumes that had risen up and seared the inside of my throat. I'd been left for dead in that wasteland and managed to survive—although the acid scars on my feet had never fully gone away. If I could withstand that, this was a walk in the park.

One thing the swamps of Morrena didn't have was a huge Raas to distract me and muddle my mind. I had to stop thinking about the gorgeous warlord, if I was going to succeed.

Never let a mark get in your head. That was what one of my academy instructors had drilled into me. And none ever had. Until now.

It didn't matter. I wasn't going to think about Raas Bron and the fact that I still needed to kill him. Not now, at least. Now I needed to contact the empire. Once they'd locked onto the Vandar horde and started their onslaught, I could use the ensuing chaos to take out the warlord.

Satisfied with my new strategy, I picked up my pace. Rounding a corner, all thoughts of the distracting male flew from my mind.

"What is this?" I walked forward, and ran my hands over the chain that surrounded the battle ring. I hadn't set foot in a practice ring in longer than I could remember. My heart pounded as I eyed the sparring weapons hanging on the inside of the circular cage.

Glancing around, I saw no one and the only sounds were the far away echoes of footsteps. The ring appeared to be in the bowels of the ship and away from the action. Surely no one would see.

I moved quickly up the short flight of stairs and entered the ring, my gaze locking on one of the sparring axes. "Let's see how hard it is to fight like a Vandar."

CHAPTER TWELVE

Bron

"We've heard from Lodvak, Raas."

My *majak's* voice pulled me from my thoughts of Alana lying naked beneath me. I shifted from one foot to the next as I stood overlooking the command deck, adjusting my cock and grasping my hands in front of me. "What do they say?"

"They welcome the human refugee." Svar glanced at me from his console, his hands gripping the curved edges. "She may either remain with them, or repatriate to her home world at a later date."

I choked out a rough laugh. "Her home world being Earth? It has long since been designated a wasteland."

Svar twitched one shoulder. "It will be her choice."

I nodded. "Good. It is done." I turned to face forward again, swallowing a hard ball of regret as I thought of the human leaving to live on an alien planet. I would most likely never see her again.

Which is a good thing, I reminded myself. *She is a distraction you never asked for and do not want.* I growled low and rested a hand on the hilt of my axe, the cool metal comforting beneath my fingers, which still buzzed hot from her touch.

"Raas?"

I looked back at my *majak*, whose eyebrows were raised. Had I growled loudly enough for him to hear? A quick glance at the other command deck officers told me that I had.

I cleared my throat. "I was thinking about the Zagrath, and how I long to spill their blood."

Several raiders rumbled their agreement, and I allowed myself an inaudible sigh, although Svar did not look so easily convinced.

The door to the command deck swished open, and Corvak stomped through them, his face set in a glower. He clicked his heels together without missing a step. "Raas, I have news of the human you will wish to hear."

"She was taken back to her quarters, yes?" I did not want the shock of walking in on her naked in my quarters again.

Corvak inclined his head while frowning. "She was, then she left."

That made me turn fully toward him. "Left? Where did she go? Did she attempt to escape?"

A brusque shake of my battle chief's head. "No, but the raider I tasked to follow her at a distance reports that she has been wandering the ship for quite some time now."

Curious. Why would a human female who claimed to be running from the empire care about exploring a Vandar warbird?

Perhaps for the same reason she was inspecting your headboard, a little voice in the back of my head whispered. *She is not a victim like she claims to be.*

"Has she found anything that should concern me?"

Corvak planted his feet wide and braced his hands on his hips. "I would have thought a female prisoner wandering the ship would be of concern, Raas."

"She is not a prisoner. She is merely a female we are transporting."

"Too bad," my battle chief grumbled so low I could barely make out his words.

I did not like Corvak's obvious disapproval of my handling of the female, but I could not fault him his opinion. There was something about the human that gave me pause. She'd struck me as both weak and scared when we'd found her, but I'd seen flashes of a tough and shrewd female beneath the bruises and tragic story. Even if she was who she claimed to be—and my doubts were growing by the second—I could not have her moving freely throughout my ship. She might not have found anything yet, but who was to say she wouldn't?

"Where is she now?" I asked.

The edges of Corvak's mouth twitched up. "She is currently in the battle ring."

I stared at him. "The holographic one?" How would a human who claimed to have been enslaved on a mining colony have any clue how to operate a holographic fighting program?

"No, Raas. Our old battle ring."

My stomach clenched. I had many memories of practicing with Raas Kratos in that iron cage. My former Raas and friend had often sparred with me while discussing his strategy or working out problems. We'd spend a good deal of time lunging at each other with sparring axes, starting when we were apprentices trying to learn how to fight, and continuing through the time that Kratos ruled the horde.

I hadn't returned to the old ring since Kratos had hung up his battle axe and named me Raas, partly because I feared it wouldn't feel the same without Kratos. I'd spent all my practice time in the new holographic battle simulator, instead of the cage that held so many memories.

"Should I have her removed and returned to her quarters?" Corvak asked when I didn't respond to him.

I drew in a breath and drummed my fingers across the carved hilt of my axe. "No. I will handle this." I met his eyes and noticed his deepening scowl. "But you may accompany me. I have a theory that might require your particular skill set."

A grin spilt Corvak's face, and he moved one hand to the handle of his weapon. "Gladly, Raas."

I gave Svar a sharp nod. "You have the horde, *majak*."

He threw back his chest and snapped his heels as I strode off the command deck with my battle chief by my side. Corvak and I didn't speak as we made our way quickly down through the ship, our steps long and our arms swinging by our sides.

My heart thrummed in my chest, anger building as I thought about the female who resided on my ship. A part of me wished to lock her in her quarters and dump her off on Lodvak as planned. It did not matter who she was, as long as she was not on my ship any longer. Another part of me needed to know the truth about her before I ridded myself of her presence. Was she truly a victim of the empire, a refugee in need as she claimed, or had she tricked me?

I squeezed the hilt of my weapon, fighting back the urge to let out a roar of frustration as I thundered down an iron staircase. The first mission of my command could not end in me being duped by a human. It was an intolerable thought, and one that made bile churn in my gut. What kind of Raas allowed himself to be tricked by a female? Kratos would never have allowed a small human like Alana to get the better of him. This thought made me tighten my grip until the bones showed white through my skin.

As we closed in on the battle ring, I held out an arm to slow Corvak and put a finger to my lips. "I do not want her to know we are watching."

He nodded and slowed his steps, and we approached with stealth and crouched in the shadows outside the iron cage.

My battle chief's report had been correct. Alana was inside the battle ring, swinging a sparring axe. Even though the blade was not sharpened, the weapon was still heavy and long—sized to accommodate a Vandar raider. Yet the human held it without drooping, slicing through the air with smooth strokes over her head.

I shifted on my haunches. She might have gained muscle through working in a mine, but she did not gain such prowess with a weapon as a miner. And she had not acquired this level of comfort in the short time she'd been inside the ring, no matter how naturally athletic she might be. I pressed my lips together as my pulse quickened. No, this female had been trained to fight.

I watched her move across the floor, her footwork agile and the movements of her arms almost mesmerizing. Although she was flushed from exertion, her face was alight with enjoyment. It was a look with which I was all too familiar. I'd seen it on my warriors' faces in the heat of battle. Not only did she know how to fight, but she also loved it.

Corvak elbowed me in the ribs, jerking his head toward the battle ring. He was right. We'd been watching long enough, and I knew what I needed to know. That is, until Alana told me the truth about herself and why she was on my warbird.

I stood and stomped up the stairs to the ring, stepping inside as she whirled toward me, her eyes wide.

"I think it's time you explained yourself." I narrowed my gaze at her. "And I strongly suggest you do not lie to me this time, female."

CHAPTER THIRTEEN

Alana

The gravelly voice startled me. I'd been so caught up in the movement of the blade as it arced through the air, balancing my weight to keep from being pitched forward from the velocity. A Vandar Battle axe—even a sparring one—was a serious weapon and one that required concentration or practice to handle. I'd spent enough hours practicing with long swords and daggers to understand how to move with a blade, but this ancient weapon was a challenge even for someone with my training.

When Raas Bron stepped into the ring across from me, my fingers faltered, as did my grip on the axe handle. The thick wood slipped from my hand and clattered to the floor.

"I didn't see you there," I started to say, the tremble in my voice not manufactured this time.

"What are you doing?" Raas Bron was not smiling, and all traces of the Vandar who'd backed away from me in his quarters with longing in his eyes had vanished.

My gaze instinctively darted to the weapon on the ground, and my fingers itched to pick it up. "I got lost."

The Raas took a step to the side like a predator beginning to circle his prey. His tail curled up off the ground, the tip quivering. "I can see that. This is not located between my quarters and yours."

My throat was thick, and my cheeks shook as I attempted a smile. I took a step away from him, circling in the opposite direction out of instinct. "I got lonely and decided to come looking for you. After all, you did leave me so suddenly."

One of his dark eyebrows lifted. "You were searching for me?" He cast his gaze around the dingy cage, shadows slinking toward the high, chain link walls around the perimeter. "Here?"

My pulse fluttered. He didn't believe me. Shit. I'd really messed things up now. Why did I let myself be tempted by the sparring ring and the weapons? I glanced again at the axe at my feet, wishing it was more than a sparring blade.

"Go ahead," he said, his voice a rumbly purr. "Pick it up."

I snapped my gaze to his and saw the challenge in his eyes. "I don't know what you—"

"Yes, you do. You're aching to reach for the weapon." His dark pupils flared, as his tail swished methodically from side to side. "So, do it." He took another sidestep and plucked a sparring axe off the wall. "You'll need it if you're going to fight me."

My pulse quickened. "Fight you?"

"That's what you want, isn't it? Someone to practice with?"

I fought the urge to let out a relieved sigh. At least he didn't suspect I was there to assassinate him. That was something. "I guess."

He nodded his head at the axe on the floor. "Then pick it up, and let's begin."

I slowly bent to retrieve the weapon, keeping my eyes fixed on him the entire time. "I should tell you that I've never used a Vandar axe before."

"Not many have." He tossed the handle of his sparring weapon from one hand to the other as if it weighed nothing. "But I suspect you will be better than you think."

As we circled each other along the rim of the ring, I eyed him. He clearly suspected me of something, but what did he know? What could he know? My name and true identity were a secret, even among all but the top leaders in the empire. To all but the very elite, I was Mantis. It would be impossible for a Vandar—even a Raas—to know anything about me.

"I am not a seasoned warrior like you, Raas." I feigned almost dropping my axe.

He grinned, but it looked more like an animal baring its teeth. "No?" He lunged for me and swept his axe wide and low, so that I had to jump to avoid my ankles being hit. "Your reflexes are as good as any raider."

I cursed myself for my instinctive response, but outwardly I giggled. "A holdover from childhood, I'm sure. Don't all children jump rope?"

He made another sudden move toward me, but I forced myself not to dodge the blow. Instead, I braced myself and prepared to let out a girlish yelp. At the last moment, he changed the trajectory of his axe, twisting it so the flat metal smacked my ass.

"Ow!" My scream was genuine.

His grin widened, and his gaze lingered on my stinging ass. "Maybe you do not have the instincts I thought you did."

I bit back the snappy response that was on the tip of my tongue and forced myself to return his smile. "I told the Raas I was not skilled in battle."

He shrugged, changing direction and coming at me from the other side. Spinning his blade rapidly, he tossed it to his other hand and darted it at me once again. Even though I could have easily defended myself with a parry of my own axe, I pretended to be flustered by his move. The slap of the flat blade to my other ass cheek made me bite my lip so hard I tasted blood.

"Having fun?" I spat out.

He bent low and shifted his weight over one knee then back to the other. "More than I had expected, although I'm disappointed you are not fighting back. I thought you'd dropped the female-in-distress act back in my quarters."

I clenched the handle of the axe. "I don't know what you're talking about. There's no act. I am a female, and I was in distress when you found me. I'm grateful to the Vandar for assisting me, but if you think I'm going to let you continue to strike me—"

"Then fight back," he growled, springing at me.

I leapt out of the way, spinning and bringing my own axe down across his back. The slap of metal against flesh made my heart beat faster, as I swiveled to face him again. Before I could draw a breath, the Raas was lunging again, this time, without his axe.

I jabbed at him but missed, and he swatted the battle axe from my grip. I dove for it, but he caught me, looping a powerful arm around my waist and flipping me over his shoulder. I tried to kick out and scissor my legs around his neck, but his hold on me was too tight. My attempts to rear up and flip him over also failed. I heaved in a series of ragged breaths as I hung upside down and the blood rushed to my head.

"You win," I said, my voice as jovial as I could make it, considering I wanted to murder him.

"I might have won the battle, human." He did not release me, but strode out of the battle ring and down the stairs. "But I have a feeling you have brought a war with you, and I intend to discover the truth of it."

The raider with the scar running down one cheek stepped out of the shadows.

"Bind her hands and feet," the Raas ordered.

I struggled in vain, my protests a series of inaudible splutters. Bind me? Was he serious?

The scarred raider's eyes were alight with an anticipation that sent ice down my spine. "Shall I hang her in my *oblek*, Raas?"

"Not your *oblek*," Raas Bron said. "I want her in my quarters."

"You can't—" I finally managed to say.

The Vandar's grip on my legs tightened. "Oh, I think I can. As I have told you before, female, I am a Raas of the Vandar. It is my duty to protect my horde by any means." His voice dropped to a deadly rumble. "Which means I can do anything to you that I wish to get the truth."

If I hadn't been hanging down his broad back, my knees might have buckled.

CHAPTER FOURTEEN

Bron

I barely noticed the startled looks as I thundered through the ship, passing gaping raiders as the female bounced on my back and pounded on my bare flesh with her small fists. I didn't slow when I reached my quarters, storming through the door and swinging her down so quickly that she nearly fell trying to regain her balance with her hands and feet bound.

"What the *klek* was that about?" She blew a strand of sweaty hair out of her eyes as she glared at me.

I tilted my head at her. "*Klek?* The Zagrath curse falls easily from your lips, human."

She started, then appeared to remember herself and where she was. "Why wouldn't it? You know I lived on a Zagrath-controlled planet. I heard plenty of Zagrath curses while working in the mines under imperial control and run by imperial soldiers."

That was a reasonable explanation, but that did not explain her battle instincts. No female who'd spent her life working in a mine would know how to fight like she had. No, those moves only came from long hours of practice and plenty of actual grappling. None of which the empire would allow for a female miner living under their rule.

"You maintain that you were running from the empire?" I asked, my gaze locked on hers and my chest still heaving both from exertion and fury.

Her eyes did not waver as she returned my stare. "It's the truth. You found me. You saw the state of my ship." She lifted her bound hands to her face and the fading bruises. "You saw what they did to me."

"Mmmm." I'd also seen the steely determination in her eyes that was not common in humans who'd lived under imperial rule. It was the same iron will I saw reflected in my raiders' faces every day.

My pulse raced as I studied the female. Every fiber of my being told me not to trust her and not to be lured by her beauty, while my body ached to taste her again. I cursed the weakness of my flesh and the swelling of my cock.

Spinning away from her so she could not see my growing arousal, I strode to the fireplace and braced my hands above the inset hearth. I focused on the cool stone even as I bit back a wave of disgust with myself. I'd doubted her earlier, yet I'd let her move freely about my warbird. It was true she hadn't found anything aside from the battle ring, but if she wasn't what she claimed to be, I could have exposed my raiders and my horde to danger. All because I'd been too flustered by my arousal to do what needed to be done.

I was Raas now, and that meant the safety of my horde came first, even above my own desires. And as a new Raas, I could not allow myself the indulgences of my predecessor. I had not led enough battles or claimed enough bounty to take a female as a prize. Even one who ignited something within me I'd never felt before. I curled my hands into fists. Especially not one who was lying to me.

I turned back to her and saw that the challenge in her gaze had softened.

She drew in a wavering breath. "Listen, I don't know how else I can convince you that I'm telling the truth. You're the one who found my ship floating in space, with no fuel and little food. It's not like I asked for a Vandar horde to board me."

Her words were persuasive, but they didn't fit *her*. Alana was no weak female, no matter what her breathy sighs and quivering voice wished to convey. No, the real her had snapped at me back in the battle ring, her words acerbic and her movements skilled.

I looked intently at her, then her words sunk in. I did have a way to make her tell the truth. It wasn't something I thought of because lying was not something Vandar did, and especially not a Raas. A Raas never lied. But he did have ways to force others to reveal the truth.

I walked closer to her. "You have told me the truth about yourself?"

She lifted her chin slightly to peer up at me. "Yes, Raas."

I bent and made quick work of untying her feet and then her hands. "Lift your arms."

She hesitated, then slowly raised them so they were straight up over her head.

I took the hem of her baggy gray shirt and swept it up and over her head in a single fast motion, leaving her chest bare and her breasts exposed.

Alana sucked in a breath as the beige skin around her nipples pebbled from the cool air. She didn't cover them with her hands, though. Instead, she kept her gaze on me as she grasped the waistband of her dark pants and shimmied them down over the swell of her hips. When the fabric pooled at her ankles, she stepped out of them and kicked them to the side.

When I'd started to undress her, I wasn't sure if I'd get the combative Alana or the temptress one, but the darkening of her eyes told me she was as eager to seduce me as she was to fight me. Her talent for adapting was impressive, and I suspected it was also something she'd practiced a great deal.

Wrapping an arm around her, I flattened a palm to the curve of her lower back and jerked her body flush to mine. Her breathing quickened, and the vein in the side of her neck throbbed.

"You know that the Vandar are raiders, and we take what we want," I murmured, lowering my lips to brush against the tip of her ear. "Since I am Raas, I can claim you as mine."

She bobbed her head up and down without speaking.

"Is that what you want?" I asked.

"Yes, Raas." Her voice cracked.

I closed my eyes and inhaled deeply, breathing in the scent of her warm skin, fresh from a fight. My hardness pressed against the heavy leather of my kilt, straining to break free. All I would need to do would be to drop my kilt and the only remaining barrier between our bodies would be gone. My body shuddered as I imagined plunging myself into her heat, and I ground my hips into her. It would be so easy to surrender to this version of her—

the version who was pliant and inviting. But I didn't want the lie. I wanted the truth.

Squeezing my eyes tight, I held her for a moment before opening them and pulling back. I looked down at her as I walked her back, my grip on her strong enough so that her feet barely touched the floor. "Close your eyes."

She gave me a sultry smile before obeying, allowing her eyes to flutter shut and her dark lashes to fan across her cheeks. "Are you taking me to bed?"

I moved quickly across the room and past the large bed, through the arched doorway and into the bathing chamber. When I reached the half-moon bathing pools, I straddled my feet on two of the stone ledges dividing the colored waters, suspending Alana over the orange pool. "There will be time for that later."

Bubbles popped around her toes and a spicy scent rose up from the pools, causing her to open her eyes. Her mouth widened in surprise as she stared at me, realizing that I had not taken her to my bed. Instead, I was dangling her over an orange, bubbling pool.

Then I dropped her.

CHAPTER FIFTEEN

Alana

The shock of hitting the water was nothing compared to the shock that he'd tricked me. My head went briefly underwater, but my feet hit the stone bottom, and I straightened my legs as water streamed down my face.

"What?…You…!" I was too livid to form a coherent sentence, as I wiped my face and spit out water. "I thought we were…"

"Not yet." The Raas stood next to the pool with his arms folded across his chest. He was not smiling, but the corner of his mouth did twitch.

"Is this supposed to be a joke?" I made my way to the edge of the pool.

"No." He flicked his fingers toward me. "And I have not told you that you can get out yet."

I fought the urge to jump out and strangle him. All in good time, I reminded myself. I still needed to convince him that I was a harmless female, which was getting harder to do with each misstep and outburst. If only he wasn't so infuriating.

I glanced down at the vivid-orange hue of the pool. It wasn't as hot as the red water sending up steam in the segment of the pool next to me, but it was bubbling and the scent wafting up was spicy and sensual.

The only perfumed water I'd ever experienced similar to this was on Grantilia, but the water had been clear, and the scent had been overwhelmingly floral. My memories of the cloying scent were unfortunately melded with thoughts of drowning the viscount to ensure the empire's successful invasion and overthrow of the ruling family. I shook these images aside and focused on the arrogant Vandar standing over me.

"Is this part of the Vandar claiming ritual?" I asked, making sure to temper my voice. I didn't want to sound as furious as I was.

Raas Bron walked to the doorway and tapped an inset panel I'd never noticed before because it was as smooth and black as the obsidian wall, the buttons also flush and flat. Soon, the bubbles popping along the surface increased, and the scent grew more intense.

"Claiming ritual?" He turned to face me, then gave a single sharp shake of his head. "Do you not enjoy bathing?"

He was up to something, but I had no idea what. Maybe he was a control freak and liked keeping me on my toes, or maybe he had a fetish about females being clean. Either way, I could play along. Soaking in a scented tub was far from the worst thing I'd had to do for my job.

I sank down so that my chin bobbed at the surface, the bubbles tickling my neck as they popped. "I do. Do all Vandar have bathing pools like this?"

"Only the Raas'." He walked to the long counter and leaned against it, stretching his muscular legs out in front of him and crossing them at the ankles. "Some of the pools have different designs, but they all have four segments with the same kinds of infused waters in each."

I glanced at the orange liquid I was soaking in. "Infused?"

"With various health benefits." He tilted his head at me. "And other properties developed by our people using ancient techniques. The waters help us heal and recover from battle, and increase our strength."

I scooped some water up in one hand and watched it drain through my fingers. "What does this water do?"

"It is used primarily for relaxing muscles."

"Well, it's working. "Although the water wasn't hot, my muscles had already uncoiled, and my legs were like noodles.

His eyes swept over me. "Good. The longer you soak, the more will be loosened."

I groped my way to the side and found a stone bench built in, and I gratefully sat. "The Vandar like to keep to the old ways, don't they?"

"We do. Even though we now live in space—the raiders, at least—we retain as much from our decimated home world as possible."

I let my neck fall back and my head loll on the stone ledge as my eyes fluttered shut. I'd never felt quite as relaxed in my life. It was as if all my worries had evaporated and every tendon in my body had been unwound.

"And what of *your* home world?" the Raas asked, his voice as soothing as a caress and as smooth as Carpithian silk.

"Faaral?" Faint memories of the planet I'd been born on danced up from the recesses of my mind. "I don't remember much. I was so young when they took me."

Somewhere in my brain, I remembered that I shouldn't speak of this, but I couldn't hold my tongue. It, too, had been freed from restraint.

There was a heavy silence, then the Raas asked, "When who took you?"

Telling the Raas the truth about my past felt completely natural. "The Zagrath, of course. They picked me out of all the children in my village. It was a great honor."

"I'm sure it was."

Memories of being wrenched away from my screaming parents made me flinch. Why was I telling this to the Raas again? Before I could answer my own question, more words spilled from me. "I didn't want to go. Not at first. And my parents didn't want me to go. I used to hear my mother's screams every time I tried to fall asleep."

"You grew up without a family?"

"The empire became my family," I said, parroting the words I'd had drilled into me. Somehow, though, it felt wrong to repeat this lie to Bron. "But it wasn't true. The instructors at the imperial academy weren't family. Their job was to break me down and build me into something they could use. The empire is not my family. I don't have a family anymore."

There was such a long silence I wondered if the Raas had left, although my eyelids were too heavy for me to open.

"I also have no family, but the horde and Raas Kratos *did* become my family." His voice was not more than a whisper.

"So, you know what it's like," I said. "To be alone."

"It is rare to ever be alone in a horde, but I do know what it is like to *feel* alone. It took a long time after my parents died for me to not to ache from their loss."

I nodded, the memories of being torn from my mother's arm rushing up and threatening to choke me. "At first, I cried myself to sleep missing my parents, but if the Zagrath caught me, they beat me. I haven't shed a tear since."

His gaze didn't leave me. "The empire took your life from you."

I shrugged. "I've been alone for so long I don't remember what anything else feels like."

"You are alone, even though you work for the empire?"

I'd never spoken to anyone about my job, but it was as if I couldn't stop myself for telling him. "I do the kind of work that you can only do alone. Not many Zagrath know I exist, even in the military."

"You're a spy?"

I laughed, the sound high and melodic. "More than a spy, Raas." I put a finger to my lips. "I'm the empire's most deadly assassin. They call me Mantis."

Another silence as I breathed in the perfumed air and wondered why I'd kept such big secrets for so long. It was freeing to talk about them. Another laugh bubbled up in my throat. I hadn't laughed a real laugh in longer than I could remember. Now, I couldn't seem to stop myself.

"And are you here to kill me?" Bron asked.

I shook a finger lazily in the air. "A very good question, Raas." I huffed out a warm breath. "That was my task, but I'm not sure if I can do it."

"No?"

I shook my head and a wave of dizziness rushed over me. "I've always been able to tell myself that the individuals I killed were bad because most of them were. Even though the empire was taking them out for a reason, they were usually greedy or cruel. But you aren't. And the raiders aren't anything like what the empire says about you. I mean, sure you're huge and terrifying, but you aren't raping and pillaging like they claim."

"You are an assassin who only kills those who deserve to die?"

I frowned at that. "Mostly. At least that's what I tell myself. It makes it easier."

The water splashed around my neck, rising higher, then there was a body brushing against my knees.

"What happens if you do not succeed in your mission?" Raas Bron pulled me out of the water and held me to his naked body. I forced my eyes to open, and his eyes were molten pools as he gazed down at me.

I stared up at him. "If I fail the empire but remain alive, I will have betrayed them. If that happens, they will send an assassin to kill *me*."

CHAPTER SIXTEEN

Bron

I swallowed hard as I looked down at the human female I held to my body—check that, the human assassin for the empire.

The scented water had done its work. The ancient oil with the rich, orange hue and slightly spicy scent was known for loosening inhibitions and lips, but even I was surprised by how effective it had been on Alana. I glanced back at the panel by the door. It hadn't hurt that I'd considerably increased the amount of oil in the water. Feeling the oil go to work on my own muscles and inhibitions, I was actually surprised she was still conscious.

She lifted a hand and pressed her slender fingers to my chest, drawing my gaze back to her. "You won't tell anyone, will you?" Her words were slurred as her eyelids drooped.

"That you're an assassin for the empire?"

Her brow furrowed even as she traced the curved marks on my chest with one finger. "That I don't want to kill the Raas."

I held her so close I was sure I could feel her heart beating. "You are sure you don't wish him dead?"

Her attention was fixed on the dark swirls climbing toward the hollow of my throat. "He isn't bad." She frowned as a tear slid from the corner of one eye. "I'm afraid he might be good."

I cupped her face and brushed the tear away with my thumb. "What if he's killed many?"

"I've killed many," she whispered.

My gaze was riveted to her finger moving languidly across my skin. "What if he's raided ships and destroyed outposts?"

She leaned in and brushed her lips against my chest. "That does not make him bad. I have met many bad creatures—and killed most of them—and I know the difference."

My skin was scorched from her touch, and my throat was thick. "But the empire will kill you if you fail."

She pressed her eyelids together briefly, then opened them and peered up at me, smiling sadly. "They were always going to kill me eventually. I think I've always known that."

"I will keep your secret."

She gave me a drowsy smile. "And I'll keep yours."

"Mine?"

"About Zendaren." Her eyelids sagged closed again, and she slumped against me, her breathing heavy. She was asleep.

Tvek. She knew about Zendaren, one of our secret Vandar colonies? I dragged a hand roughly through my hair as I held her with one hand looped around her back. Now what? I'd unmasked her true identity, but I'd also revealed her painful past. She wasn't working for the Zagrath because she was one of them, or even because she believed in their cause. She'd been ripped from her family and raised in some kind of brutal academy, made into a killer by the same bastards who'd ruined her life in the first place. She was a victim of their cruelty as much as anyone the empire used for its own greedy purposes. And now, she also knew a secret about my people.

I brushed a wet strand of hair from her forehead, and my heart pounded as I thought about what the Zagrath had done to her. I would make them pay for taking a child and destroying her life and her future. I didn't know where the Zagrath academy was located, but I would find it and destroy it and liberate all of the children who had been snatched from their life.

I was filled with a sense of purpose as I thought about my new mission, my pulse quickening as I imagined the damage I would inflict on the Zagrath. Then my stomach clenched into a tight ball. I had been right to suspect her and voice my suspicions to my closest officers. She wasn't what she'd pretended to be, and she'd cleverly tricked her way onto my ship. My instincts had been right about that. But I also couldn't tell Svar and Corvak what I'd learned. Not if I wanted to protect Alana.

I groaned as I reached down and scooped her into my arms, water streaming from her body. Even though I'd just learned that she was on my ship to assassinate me, I couldn't bear the thought of her being punished by Corvak. And if I told my battle chief what I'd discovered, there would be no choice but to let him interrogate her in his *oblek*. Anything else would be betraying the Vandar, and our mission to destroy the empire. Any other action, and I would be failing in my duty to protect my horde and my people.

Taking long steps from the bathing pools, I stood for a moment on the glossy black, floor as scented water puddled around my feet. I didn't bother to use the pressurized air to dry us as I knew it would wake her. Instead, I carried her into the main room, pulling a length of cloth from an inset drawer and tossing it on the bed before laying her on top.

The sight of her naked body made my cock harden, but I wrapped her quickly in the thick fabric. She'd passed out from the intoxicating effects of the oil, and I didn't want her this way.

But you do want her.

I turned away quickly, striding naked away from the bed and the female who made such a mess of my thoughts. I took out another length of fabric, wrapping it around my waist and trying to ignore how my hardness tented the makeshift kilt.

But I couldn't ignore what I'd learned. That would be suicide, especially if she had second thoughts about sparing me. But I'd never live with myself if I allowed her to be tortured or killed.

I stormed across the room until I was gazing out the wide wall overlooking space. What would Kratos do, I wondered? He'd never been known to show mercy. Until he'd met his human female, that is. Then he'd spared her life and claimed her as his prize—part of the spoils of war the Vandar took as our right.

I'd been adamant that I would not do the same, that I wouldn't take Alana as my captive.

"That was before you learned her secret," I said to myself, casting a quick glance at the female still sleeping in my bed. "That was before you discovered she's a sworn enemy of the Vandar."

I had no choice. If I wanted to keep her secret safe—and keep her from telling anyone about Zendaren—I would have to claim her as mine. I would have to tell my most trusted officers that I'd decided I wanted her to warm my bed, and we wouldn't be delivering her to the planet of Ludvok.

I pressed one flat palm against the glass, welcoming the coolness on my hot flesh. Would Svar and Corvak—the two Vandar raiders who knew me best on the ship—be convinced by my words after I'd insisted I did not want the female—that I had no desire to take any female? Svar might take me at my word. He was my *majak*, after all.

But Corvak would not. He'd always been more suspicious. His position as battle chief demanded he see danger around every corner and a deception lurking in every heart. It was one of the reasons he was such a skilled interrogator. Not only that, but he'd also seen Alana in the battle ring and shared the suspicions that had just been borne out by my questioning. I would need more than empty words to convince him I'd changed my mind. I would have to convince him that I was so overcome with desire that I could not give her up. That she fucked me so well that I preferred only her in my bed instead of the pleasurers we frequented.

I twisted to look at her again, her dark hair spilling across the crimson sheets and my mouth went dry. That would not be the hard part. The hard part would be telling Alana that she now belonged to me—and she would not be leaving my ship.

CHAPTER SEVENTEEN

Alana

The dull ache of my head woke me, and I touched a hand to my temple as I opened my eyes. Where was I again? I peered through the dimly lit room, the only light emanating from the blue flames in the wall fireplace.

"That's right," I mumbled to myself. "The Raas' quarters."

There was no sound, save the crackling of the fire and the constant hum of the ship's engines. The Raas must have slept somewhere else because as I sat up, I realized I was alone in the huge bed. The slippery sheet fell to my waist, and I pulled it back up as I glanced down. Alone in bed, and very naked.

Swinging my feet over the side of the bed, I rubbed my head. When had I undressed, and where were my clothes?

My eyes caught on the arched doorway leading to the bathing pools, and my stomach clenched. *The bathing pools.* My last memory was sitting in the fragrant water and talking to Raas Bron. Words floated through my mind as I tried desperately to recall what I'd told him.

He'd been asking me questions about myself and my past. I cringed as I remembered telling him that I was born on Faaral. So much for my cover story of being a miner escaping the empire.

"Fuck." I stood so quickly my head swam, but I ignored the pain and the surge of nausea as my gaze locked on the heavy, iron door. If the Raas knew I wasn't who I claimed to be, I needed to get the hell off his ship. He might have left me alone for now, but I doubted I would be afforded my freedom for much longer.

I wrapped the sheet around me and walked across the room as quickly as I could, a train of fabric swishing behind me like a tail. I couldn't even worry about the mission that I'd clearly have to abandon. Now my only goal was to get off the Vandar ship alive. I'd have to worry about the repercussions once there was no chance I'd be tortured to death by the raiders or put out an airlock. The Vandar did not have a reputation for mercy, and I'd heard rumors they didn't even have a brig because they never took anyone alive, or waited to mete out punishment.

When I reached the door, I slapped my hand on the panel to one side. The round metal door didn't part like it normally did. I pressed harder, but it didn't budge.

"No no no no no no," I whispered, as I let the sheet fall and tried to wedge my fingers at the seam of the door and pull the two sides apart.

Nothing happened. They were locked. I leaned my palms against the door and heaved in a breath. I wouldn't be escaping from the Vandar, after all. Was the Raas' menacing battle chief on his way now to take me? Would there be any kind of trial or would they kill me immediately?

Bile churned in my gut, and I squeezed my eyes tight. How had I been so stupid? I knew better than to reveal information about myself. I thought back to talking with the Raas. But it had felt so right to answer his questions. Actually, it had seemed like an impossibility not to answer them.

Regret joined my growing sense of dread. Would I see Raas Bron before I was executed? Even though he was the reason I'd failed to fulfill my mission, I wished I could see him again.

"Don't be stupid, Alana," I said, lifting my head and trying to gather my courage. "He wouldn't want to see you."

"I hope you aren't talking about me."

The voice came out of the darkness, causing me to spin and scramble for the sheet puddled on the floor. "What the hell?!"

I squinted toward the glass wall, my eyes adjusting to the darkness. The figure sitting at the long table stood, and the Raas walked slowly toward me.

Even though I was standing at the door, I instinctively took a step back as the massive warrior advanced on me, and I bumped against the cold metal. "How long have you been there? Were you watching me sleep?"

"I was waiting for you to wake."

I'd been thoroughly trained in hand-to-hand combat, but even I wasn't brash enough to attack the huge alien while wearing nothing but a sheet and nursing some kind of weird hangover. Not that I wanted to attack the Raas. As bizarre as it seemed, the sight of him provoked a fluttering of my pulse and throbbing between my legs, instead of murderous instincts.

When he was towering over me, I forced myself to meet his serious gaze. "So, you can tell me my fate?"

He inclined his head slightly. "You could say that."

My heart pounded so hard I put a hand to my chest. I'd been trained for everything, but the reality of death still sent fear clawing at my throat. "Can you do it quick? I don't know what the Vandar usually do to prisoners, but I'd rather not be tortured before you kill me."

"Kill you?" Bron closed his hand over mine. "You think I was waiting for you to wake so I could kill you?" He shook his head. "If I wanted you dead, you would not have lived through the night."

"Oh." That was comforting, I guess. Maybe I hadn't told the Raas the truth about me. Maybe I'd dreamt it all, and my cover was still intact. "Are we still en route to Ludvok?"

He tightened his hand around mine, pulling it toward him. "I do not think it would be fair to the citizens of that planet to drop off a Zagrath spy and assassin, do you?"

I attempted to jerk my hand away, but he held firm. Then he grabbed my other wrist, causing me to lose my grip on the sheet entirely. It cascaded to a heap at my feet, leaving me naked and struggling to get away from him.

"There is no point in fighting me, female." His voice was so calm it startled me into stopping my flailing. "I told you I have no intention of killing you for your treachery."

"It wasn't personal," I said, my voice cracking as I lifted my chin to meet his gaze. "I don't know if I could have killed you, anyway."

"I know." His grip on my wrists loosened, but I didn't move. "That is why I'm not going to tell my officers what I know about you."

"You aren't?"

"If any other Vandar learns the truth about you, I will have no choice but to turn you over to my battle chief for interrogation." He sighed. "Anything else would be a betrayal of my people."

"Why would you help me?" My breath hitched in my chest. "Especially since I was sent here to kill you."

He pulled me until I bumped against his bare chest. "You are as much a casualty of the empire as my people. Just as their actions made us take to space and become raiders, the Zagrath forced you to be a killer. But neither of us need to let our enemy define us. Only we get to decide who we are."

I shook my head, a familiar wave of inevitable despair washing over me. "I don't know anything but killing for the empire. It's who I am."

"Not anymore. Now you are mine."

I opened my mouth to argue, but he crushed his lips to mine, wrapping his arms around me and pinning my wrists to the small of my back. My protests were swallowed by his hard kiss, which sent shivers of pleasure ricocheting through my body. When he tore his mouth away just as suddenly, I was left gasping.

Raas Bron's gaze was blazing as he stared down at me, his breathing ragged. "I will give you a choice the empire never gave you. You can choose to be mine and be given all the protections of the Raas or you can answer for your crimes."

My heart skittered like a Garnithian water bug dancing across a pond. "What do you mean 'be yours?'"

"The only way I can keep you on board without my motives being questioned is if I claim you as part of the spoils of war my people claim as raiders." He lowered his mouth so that his lips buzzed against my neck. "You would be my mate and the property of the Vandar."

I inhaled sharply. "Until we stop somewhere, and you release me?"

"No." His arms tightened around my back. "Once you are mine, there is no going back. You will remain on my ship and in my bed."

"You could pretend you didn't know. Drop me off as planned and go about your way."

His gaze bored into me. "But didn't you say that if you failed the empire would send someone to kill you?"

"But I wouldn't be your problem." I attempted to step back, desperate to put some distance between us. "You could walk away without feeling guilty that you had anything to do with what happens to me."

He shook his head. "I can't do that."

I groaned. "No one told me that Vandar were so stubborn, or that they had some outdated sense of chivalry."

"You believe me wanting to protect you is outdated?"

I lifted my chin to meet his eyes. "I can take care of myself. I'm not your responsibility."

"You're wrong about that." He moved my hands behind me and leaned closer, so I had to bow my back to stare up at him. "I have already claimed you as mine. You *are* mine."

"Just because you say something—"

He jerked me so I was flush to him. "The words of a Vandar Raas have power. I have claimed you and given you the protection of all the Vandar warriors under my command."

I sucked in a breath, his molten gaze making my legs weak. There was an honesty in his gaze that took my breath away. For the first time in as long as I could remember, someone wanted to help me, and it wasn't because they would be getting a bag of coin for their troubles. I didn't know why he was so set on saving me, but my gut told me that this Vandar was worthy of my rarely bestowed trust.

"You aren't afraid I'll kill you while we sleep?"

He chuckled low, as he reached down and swept me into his arms. "Who said anything about sleep?"

CHAPTER EIGHTEEN

Bron

I carried Alana to the bed and let her fall back as I released her arms.

She propped herself on her elbows and scooted back. "When you said you would claim me, I didn't think you meant now."

She didn't attempt to cover her naked body, and part of me wished she was some shy creature who embarrassed easily. Keeping my gaze from the swell of her breasts and the bare folds of her sex was a challenge. One I was failing at, as my blood fired, and my cock swelled. I forced my eyes to focus on her face and the pink hue of her cheeks, instead of the arousing flush of her chest. "You had no issue with timing when you attempted to seduce me earlier."

Her cheeks mottled a deeper pink, and her gaze shifted away from me. "That was because it was part of my plan."

"You think this is not?"

She cut her eyes back to me, narrowing them as she looked up at me. "You expect me to believe you want to fuck me because of some plan?"

I bent over her and braced one hand on the bed, sinking into the softness. "My plan is to claim you so you will not be declared an enemy of the Vandar and held in my battle chief's *oblek*. Once you are mine, you will have my protection. But that is not why I *want* to fuck you."

Her dark pupils swallowed the lighter iris of her eyes. "No?"

I shook my head as the vein on the side of her neck throbbed. "I've never fucked an assassin before, especially not one who wanted to kill me."

"And I've never fucked a mark who knew he was a mark."

"Is that why they call you the Mantis?" I lowered my head and inhaled deeply at her neck, detecting remnants of the scented oil clinging to her skin. "You fuck your victim before you kill them?"

She quickly wrapped her legs around my waist, jerking hard and flipping me onto the bed beside her. Another hard move and she'd rolled on top of me, straddling my waist and pressing her hands to my chest. She smiled down at me, twitching one shoulder. "Everyone deserves to die happy, even the guilty."

She was faster than I'd given her credit for—and stronger. I reached up and grasped her waist, my large hands spanning across her belly. "I agree."

I lifted her up and tossed her to one side, where she landed on her belly. Before she could push up, I'd flipped on top of her and pinned her down, my hands flattening hers over her head. She bucked against me, but I avoided the sharp movement of her head. I pressed my own head to the side of hers to keep her from trying to head butt me again. "Why do you fight me?"

Her breathing was heavy, and she wiggled beneath me. "I'm used to being on top."

Her struggling made my cock ache as it strained against the leather of my battle kilt. "I'm sure you are, but you've never been with a Vandar Raas before, have you?"

She huffed out a breath. "You're still a male. You aren't so different from the rest."

"We'll see." I nipped at her neck, and she yelped, thrashing beneath me. I released her hands and sat back, allowing her to turn onto her back.

She put a hand to the flesh I'd bitten and glared at me. "Do Vandar like to mark their conquests or something?"

I glanced at the smooth flesh of her breasts, imagining dark swirls curling across it. "If I mark you, you will know."

Her eyes flashed but then dropped to my marks. "Are those your mating marks?"

Her comment reminded me that she'd studied up on my people to better infiltrate us and assassinate me. I stood and backed away from her. "You do not need to worry yourself about those."

"I know humans have gotten them. Word reached the empire about Raas Kratos' mate."

"She is his Raisa," I said, folding my arms over my chest. "And she is with child."

Alana sat up, leaning back on her hands. "And you don't think you risk that by screwing me?"

She clearly hadn't learned enough about the Vandar. "Just because I fuck you doesn't mean you would become heavy with child. Only a Vandar's true mate can take his mating marks or become pregnant."

She eyebrows lifted. "So, you have to find your one fated mate or you can't have children? That's rough."

"Rough?"

She shrugged. "What if you fall for someone who never takes your marks?" She studied me. "And what about me? You said I'd never leave this ship or your bed. Does that mean you'll never take a Vandar mate? That you're stuck with me even if I never get your marks or get knocked up?"

I hadn't thought beyond my instinct to protect her and keep her from the vengeful grasp of Corvak and keep her knowledge out of the hands of the empire, but she was right. If I claimed her as my war prize, I would have to give her up one day or live with the reality of never having a legacy. Unless she ended up taking my marks, which I knew was possible for a human but doubtful for a trained assassin who associated sex with murder.

I eyed the dark-haired beauty on the bed, her muscles tensed as if ready to battle me again. Could this imperial spy possibly be my one true mate? It seemed impossible.

She must have read the expression on my face because she shook her head slowly, her shoulders sagging. "I appreciate you trying to help me, but I'm never going to get your marks or become your one and only. It's nothing personal, but I'm not wired for true love or fate or any of that crap. It may work for your people but it's never going to happen with me."

Even though she was probably right, hearing her state it so baldly made anger flare in my belly. I strode to her until I loomed over her on the bed. "You would rather I put you out an airlock?"

"Maybe you should," she whispered. "It's not like I don't deserve it."

My throat tightened. She would rather be killed than be my mate? I growled low, cursing my bad luck. Kratos had taken a female who'd been shy and scared and eager to please him. I'd taken a female who had been tasked to kill me and did not believe in any of the truths my people held dear. So far, being Raas was not what I'd imaged it to be.

I dragged a hand across my brow, kneading the furrowed flesh. I'd already promised to protect her and keep her secrets. There was only one way to do that and keep my officers from being suspicious. If I wanted to keep my horde and keep the female from being executed, there was no other choice.

"It does not matter." I turned from her. "I offered you protection, and a Vandar Raas does not go back on his word."

"Even if it means you're stuck with a woman who will never be your true mate? Come on, there has to be another way."

"There is not," I snapped, then pushed down the bitter taste of regret and took long steps toward the door. "It is done."

CHAPTER NINETEEN

Bron

The clatter of my footsteps echoed on the iron walkway as I stormed to my command deck. Raiders clicked their heels together as they passed but I barely glanced at them, grunting in acknowledgement as I barreled through the ship.

What had I done? Had I gone mad?

I scraped a hand through my hair and thought back to my days as *majak*. If Kratos had come to me with the same problem, how would I have advised him? A frustrated growl rumbled low in my throat. Kratos never would have taken an assassin under his protection. Even if it was an alluring female in which he wanted to bury his cock. Would he?

It didn't matter. I'd made a promise I couldn't revoke. Now I had to convince my most trusted officers that I'd done an about face and decided to claim the female instead of depositing her on Ludvok.

I despised the thought of lying to my own raiders, but I also knew that the truth would mean pain and possibly death for Alana. Despite the fact that she'd been sent to kill me, I couldn't stomach the idea of her being hurt.

Gritting my teeth, I entered the command deck and swept my gaze across the bare-chested raiders standing at their consoles. Svar pivoted toward me, his back straightening when he saw who it was.

He tapped his heels sharply. "Raas. Was your interrogation successful?"

"Do you require my assistance?" Corvak asked, stepping away from his own console.

"It was," I hesitated as I searched for the right word, "productive."

Svar angled his head at me, but before he could ask another question, I fixed my eyes on the view screen.

"Our destination is no longer Ludvok," I said, clasping my hands behind my back.

Svar and Corvak were silent as they stared at me.

"We are changing course, Raas?" Svar finally asked. "We will not be dropping off the female on the planet?"

I gave a curt shake of my head. "We will not be dropping the female off anywhere." I rocked back on my heels. "I have decided to claim her as one of the spoils of our raiding mission."

Several heads swiveled toward me. These raiders had been on board when Raas Kratos had taken a female as his war prize. There had been murmurs about his intentions then, although it was acknowledged that a Raas could take any female—especially one in league with the empire—as his captive. The only difference with Alana was that my crew believed her to be running from the empire, not in league with them.

"You are keeping the female?" Corvak asked, his scowl dark and fierce.

I attempted to shrug lightly. "She pleases me. Why should I give her up? Is it not the prerogative of a Raas to claim any female he wants? Are we not raiders?"

A rumble of agreement passed through the command deck with some raiders stomping their feet.

Corvak bowed his head slightly. "Of course, Raas. You may claim any female you wish, but I thought you had suspicions about this one and about her actions."

I waved a hand. "I was wrong. She was merely curious."

"But she fought you in the battle ring," he said, lowering his voice.

I grinned at Corvak. "I prefer a female who fights back. Are you not the same, battle chief?"

His lip curled, no doubt thinking of the pleasurers he selected when we visited the pleasure planets—athletic alien females whom he chased through the houses before they allowed themselves to be caught. "I did not know you enjoyed that, Raas."

"Is there a Vandar who does not enjoy a challenge? Especially since we have not tasted battle in many rotations?"

Svar cleared his throat. "If we are no longer taking the human to Ludvok, to where should we set a course, Raas?"

I had not thought that far. If our mission was no longer to rid ourselves of the female on the alien planet, where should we go?

Corvak's head dropped as his console beeped. "We might not need to set a new course, Raas."

I exhaled even as the back of my neck tingled at the barely controlled excitement in my battle chief's voice. "What is it?"

"An imperial cruiser, Raas." Corvak looked up and grinned. "Flying alone."

"That was a tactical error," Svar said.

"It's not uncommon for imperial cruisers to fly alone in this part of the sector," Corvak reminded us. "Our horde is rarely here."

"Then bad luck for them." I squared my stance as I face the view screen. "Show me."

A few taps of Corvak's console made the image of the Zagrath ship appear on the massive glass extending across the widest part of the command deck. All the officers snapped their heads up and stared, letting out low rumbles and shifting their feet in eager anticipation.

The dull gray hull of the chunky vessel looked intact, and the ship appeared to be cruising at a steady speed. This was no injured freighter.

I curled my fingers around the hilt of my battle axe. "What do your sensors tell you?"

"Imperial cruiser with a small crew. Standard weapon capability and fully operational shields." Corvak's gaze was fixed on the screen, and his dark eyes flashed. "There is no reason we should not be able to overtake them easily, Raas."

"Good." The possibility of battle fired my blood and stoked my need for victory, even if the ship was modest. "Assemble a raiding party and alert the other horde ships. I will meet you on the hangar bay."

Corvak clicked his heels, tapping quickly on his screen then walking briskly from the command deck.

I shifted my gaze to my *majak*. "Ready to spill some Zagrath blood?"

He clutched the top of his own axe. "I am always ready to bring glory to Vandar."

As we walked astride off the command deck, my lips curled into a snarl. Now more than ever, I needed a raiding mission to remind me of my duties as Raas and my oath to crush the empire. Especially since I harbored one of their spies in my quarters.

CHAPTER TWENTY

Alana

I waited until he'd left to retrieve the sheet from the floor, wrapping it around myself as I searched for my clothes. My memory was hazy, but hadn't I taken them off in the main room? Since they were clearly not here, maybe I'd dropped them near the pools.

I poked my head through the arched doorway but didn't spot my discarded clothing anywhere on the shiny, obsidian floors or counter. Glancing at the vividly colored water made me cringe as I turned away, the perfumed scent a sharp reminder. If I hadn't been so relaxed maybe I wouldn't have spilled all my secrets.

"And then I wouldn't be stuck on a Vandar warbird."

I shouldn't be complaining. Any other alien I'd been trying to kill wouldn't have thought twice before throwing me in a cell or out an airlock. I wasn't sure exactly why the Raas was so determined to save me, but I wasn't going to question it too much. Not when the alternative was pretty grim.

I shivered as I remembered the battle chief with the scar running down his face and the menacing look in his eyes. That guy would have no problem punishing me. Then I thought about the imperial forces. If they discovered I'd failed to kill the Raas, they'd treat me even less kindly than the Vandar.

"I guess I have no choice," I whispered, pulling the silky sheet tighter around me and attempting not to think of the huge warlord who'd claimed me as his property. Part of me bristled at the idea of belonging to anyone, but another part of me couldn't deny the intense reactions his touch provoked. My pulse tripped at the mere memory of his lips brushing my skin.

"Come on, Alana." I stamped a bare foot on the hard floor. "Get a grip. You're not some innocent virgin being swept off your feet. You've had plenty of guys before."

And killed most of them, a little voice reminded me. And stayed with none longer than a few rotations. The thought of staying on the Vandar ship indefinitely caused panic to flutter in my chest. I never stayed anywhere long enough to get attached or be remembered. It was part of the job. And now this Vandar warlord was telling me I had to stay? Permanently?

"As if," I mumbled as the engines of the ship slowed, and I grabbed the doorframe for balance. Was the Vandar ship stopping because we'd reached the planet the Raas claimed he wasn't going to leave me on? No, that would have been too fast.

My skin prickled with fear. My highly tuned instincts were telling me that something was wrong—and my gut was never wrong about these things.

I gathered the sheet tighter around me and stomped to the door, pounding on it until it opened. The guard outside raised an eyebrow at me, but didn't comment on my attire.

"Why are we slowing?" I asked.

He frowned at me, clearly debating if he should disclose any information to me.

I sighed and tried to give him my most endearing smile. "Come on." I waved a hand at my sheet. "Do you really think I'm a threat?"

His frown didn't fade. "It's a raiding mission. It won't take long. Go back inside and wait for the Raas."

"A raiding mission? Is it an imperial fleet?"

His frown hardened. "If it was a fleet there would be red alerts and the sounds of battle."

"So, a single ship?" The hairs on the back of my neck stood on end. This was not an accident. The horde had come across another imperial ship so soon because the empire had planned it this way.

The guard grunted, clearly done answering my questions and maybe not pleased with himself for telling me anything at all. "You should wait inside. The Raas will return soon."

I backed up and allowed the doors to shut again, my mind racing with possibilities. What was the strategy? I was willing to bet my life this was part of some imperial war game. The Zagrath rarely sent out solo ships. The question was, were they doing this to save me or kill me?

Since my ship had been destroyed along with the tracked cargo, they'd lost all ability to track me. I'd also been unable to send any sort of transmission. They must think I was either dead or captured. Either way, they were now sacrificing one of their ships so they could lure the horde into showing itself or attacking.

Then what? I paced a long path from one end of the room to the other, the sheet dragging behind me like a tail. Having the Vandar raid their ship wouldn't make it possible to hunt down the horde, and it certainly wouldn't guarantee that the Raas was killed. It wasn't like the empire had invisibility shielding or could hide a fleet from view. Vandar sensors would pick up on approaching vessels and be able to vanish like smoke.

"It's something more subtle," I whispered to myself, nibbling my bottom lip as I thought.

What would I do if I needed to find a captured spy? My gut coiled into a hard ball. I'd send in another spy.

"Fuck me sideways," I said. That was it. They were using the imperial ship as a way to lure the Vandar into sending raiding ships. Once the raiding ships were on board, the spy would manage to sneak onto one and return with the raiders. Then he'd be on the warbird. I knew in my gut that this was what the empire was doing because it was something I'd done before, just not against the Vandar.

One of my most notorious missions had been when I'd snuck onto a pirate ship that had attacked an imperial vessel. While the pirates had terrorized the crew, killing them all, I'd climbed onto their transport and made it back to their main vessel. There I'd systematically murdered all of the alien mercenaries without them ever figuring out they had an imperial spy in their midst.

I groaned. If I was right, the empire was using my own playbook against me.

I strode to the inset dresser, grabbing one of the hanging kilts and pulling it on. It was huge, so I rolled it up around my waist until it stopped slipping down my hips. I opened a drawer below and pawed through it until I found a baggy tunic. I pulled it on and tied it in a knot at my waist as my mind whirred.

The Zagrath were definitely coming. They were coming to finish the job I hadn't. I bristled at the thought of another imperial assassin on the ship, not only because I hated the thought of my competition, but because I knew now I couldn't let them succeed. I could not stand by and let them murder Bron. Not when he'd put himself on the line for me.

The heat prickling my skin was like a fever that made my heart beat unevenly and my mouth go dry. There were more reasons that I couldn't bear the thought of the Raas being killed, but I didn't want to think too hard about why the alien warlord provoked such unwanted feelings of desire and longing in me. All I knew for sure was that he'd been the only person to put himself at personal and professional risk for me in…well, ever. Foiling the empire's plot against him was the least I could do, especially since I'd been plotting to kill him myself.

Once I'd dressed, I forced myself to take in a long breath to steady the relentless drumbeat of my heart. The question was, who had they sent after me, and could I find them before they assassinated Raas Bron and then me for failing to kill him first?

CHAPTER TWENTY-ONE

Bron

I let out a roar as my raiding party spilled onto the imperial ship, shields braced, and our axes poised to rain terror on the enemy soldiers. We'd used our invisibility shielding the slip onto their hangar bay without trigging any alarms or sensors, but we had no desire to hide our attack now.

The Zagrath cruiser wasn't close to the size of one of our warbirds, but it was large enough to hold the two raiding ships we'd just landed in the hangar bay as well as a pair of imperial shuttlecrafts. A member of the deck crew who looked shocked at our appearance ducked out the wide arched doors when he saw us. Moments later, red lights flashed overhead, illuminating the walls and making my fellow raiders' faces appear even more menacing in the crimson glow.

We advanced as a single unit, our shields locked in front of us, as we moved swiftly through the ship. The imperial ship was like all the others we'd seen—bright, enclosed corridors that now pulsed red as wailing alarms echoed off the sleek walls. For as many enemy ships as I'd raided, the brightness always made me flinch as I wondered why the aliens chose glaring lights and blaring white surfaces that made my eyes ache to look at them.

"Should we break off, Raas?" Svar asked as we came to a fork in the corridor.

Remembering the layout of the last imperial cruise we'd stormed, I nodded to a pair of raiders. "Clear the right passage then return to us."

One of the raiders gave a sharp nod. "No prisoners?"

I thought of the merciless empire that had destroyed the home world I'd never seen, subjugated millions, and kidnapped Alana, forcing her into a life as a killer. "No prisoners," I growled.

Rounding a corner, we were rushed by two helmeted soldiers firing their blasters. The blasts ricocheted off the thick iron of our shields, then Svar swung his shield up to slam into both of their arms and send their weapons flying from their hands. Without even a moment to register the shocked looks on their faces, I sliced my battle axe through the air and lopped off their heads. Blood splattered the pristine walls as the helmets cartwheeled through the air and landed with decisive thud.

Screams came from behind us—an indication our pair of raiders had found imperial fighters—but we stepped over the lifeless bodies and moved forward. I glanced at the slick blade of my axe, the dripping blood making my pulse dance. It had been too long since I'd handed out Vandar justice, and my chest swelled at the sense that all was as it should be.

We passed more empty rooms as we moved through the ship, Svar quickly dispatching another pair of soldiers without one of them even firing off a single round.

As the lifeless bodies dropped to the floor, I grinned at him. "Well done, *majak*."

His face was alight with excitement, and his eyes burned with vengeance. "It feels good to strike a blow to the enemy."

I knew how he felt. Every dead Zagrath was one less soldier who would enslave alien civilizations or occupy peaceful planets. The fact that they were faceless creatures in helmets made it even easier.

When we reached a central space in the ship with corridors leading off it like spokes of a wheel, I sent pairs of raiders down each one.

"Strip the ship of any weapons or technology," I told them before they rushed off down their assigned corridors. "We need to know what the enemy is up to. Once you've taken what we need, return to the warbird and we will follow once we've dispatched the command crew."

They clicked their heels and moved off, still in defensive formation. Svar and the remaining two raiders stayed with me to breach the command deck, and we moved swiftly and wordlessly toward our target. After raiding countless Zagrath vessels, their layout was as familiar to me as the schematics of my own warbird. It helped that the ships were simplistic and consistent in design. All of their freighters were alike, as were all their cruisers.

We took out a small complement of soldiers as we got closer to the command deck, leaving them sprawled on the floor with their useless blasters still in their hands. It was almost too easy, I thought, as we paused outside the sealed doors leading to the command deck. Although we were breathing heavy and our axes were slippery with enemy blood, the ship had not been prepared for an attack and the soldiers had seemed barely able to defend themselves.

"The enemy forces are less and less of a challenge," Svar said, giving voice to my thoughts.

"Perhaps they cannot train them as fast as we can kill them," I said, although the ease of our mission stole some of the glory.

I motioned for two raiders to pry open the doors, then we all rushed onto the bridge, shields high in preparation for a final stand from the enemy crew. When there was no volley of blaster fire, I lowered my shield to study the command deck officers.

There were only two Zagrath males in crisp smoke-blue uniforms, both of them so fresh-faced I was surprised to see they had stubble on their cheeks. One sat at a console and was clearly the pilot, and the other stood with his shoulders thrown back and his chin jutting up. If he was the captain, he was the youngest one I'd ever seen.

Svar emitted a disgusted groan, dropping his battle axe to his side. "You are the ship's senior officers?"

The captain who was little more than a boy lifted his chin higher. "I am Captain Jernen."

I glanced at Svar, whose brow was furrowed, then back at the imperial captain. "How long have you been captain?"

He hesitated. "I was promoted just before this mission."

Fear tingled at the back of my neck as I approached the captain. I towered over the shaking Zagrath, the blood of his fellow soldiers dripping from the curve of my blade onto his black boots. "Tell me, Captain, are we your mission?"

His gaze snapped to mine too quickly. It was all the answer I needed. This single imperial ship with its crew of untrained fighters and green officers was a trap. I wasn't sure how, but the gnawing in my gut told me it had to do with Alana. And I'd left her alone on my ship.

I turned and ran off the enemy command deck.

CHAPTER TWENTY-TWO

Alana

I had to get away from the Vandar guard so I could go hunting for the imperial spy. They were either on board or they would be soon. I could feel it.

I pounded on the door to the Raas' quarters again. The door swished open, and the guard faced me with his hands on his hips. His broad chest muscles were flexed as he stared me down, one hand shifting to the top of his battle axe. "What?"

I debated how to approach him. Should I try to convince him that the horde was in trouble? That probably wouldn't fly since all the raiders on board still believed I was a victim of the empire. Convincing him I knew what I was talking about because I was actually an imperial spy would not go well for me.

"I need to talk to the Raas," I said. "Is he back yet?"

The guard narrowed his gaze at me. "You will see him when he returns to his quarters. Not before."

I huffed out a breath. Why were all Vandar males so infuriatingly stubborn? "Listen," I said, attempting to make my voice more persuasive. "It's about the raiding mission. I have a bad feeling that—"

"The Vandar conduct raiding missions on imperial ships all the time." He gave me a patronizing look. "It's the mission of our hordes."

"Yes, but—" I started to argue with him but then his face went slack, and he dropped to his knees.

I jumped out of the way as his huge body slammed onto the steel floor with an echoing thud. It only took me a moment to see the blade sticking out of his back and to dodge quickly at the flash of movement to one side.

I spun, scanning the open air corridor and assuming a battle stance.

"So, you haven't forgotten who you are." The deadly voice slid down my spine as he stepped out of the shadows.

"Krennick." I uttered the word like a curse. Of all the imperial assassins, why had they sent him?

The human had dark hair, and a wiry frame that was sheathed completely in black, which made him easy to lose in the dimness of the Vandar ship. His eyes were as black as the rest of him and as cold as an ice planet.

"How long has it been, Mantis?" He gave me a smile that made me shiver.

"Since the academy."

"Right." He nodded leisurely, as if we were two schoolmates catching up on old times. The reality was he'd always despised me, especially since I'd bested him at almost everything while we were in training. "That was a long time ago."

Not long enough, I thought, my gaze raking over his body. He didn't appear to be holding a weapon, but when it came to imperial assassins, looks were deceiving, and I suspected he had plenty of weapons attached to him, just carefully hidden.

"Why are you here, Krennick?" I didn't actually have any doubt why the empire had sent him, but I did need to buy some time.

He glanced down at the dead Vandar and then past me into the Raas' quarters. "To finish the job you could not."

"You presume too much."

His slippery gaze traveled down the length of me, taking in the Vandar clothes I'd adjusted to fit my smaller body. "I don't think so. You even look like them."

My competitive nature hated the suggestion that he'd been sent in because I had failed at something. I never failed. The truth was, I had never even tried to kill the Raas. Not that I was going to argue that to *him*.

"You should go before you blow my cover and ruin my entire mission," I snapped, my ire that he was encroaching on my mission flaring.

"You really expect me to believe that you've been on the enemy ship and in the warlord's private chamber for all this time and still haven't figured out how to slit his throat?" He made tsk-ing noises. "You've never lingered over a mission before."

"I'm not lingering over this one," I said. "But this mission requires more time. And I can't pull it off if you blow my cover."

"Your mission is over." A smile curled his thin lips. "As are you, Mantis. The empire doesn't tolerate operatives who've turned. Or gone soft."

My fingers tingled, but I fought the urge to fist them and tip him off. "You think I've gone soft?"

"The Raas lives, which means you couldn't kill him," he hissed, flicking a blade out of a pouch on his pants. "A failure I'm here to correct. As soon as I deal with your treachery." Without another word, he flung the blade at me.

I ducked, hearing it whiz by my ear and embed in the steel doorframe behind me. Shit. He wasn't messing around. Spinning, I wrenched the blade from where it had landed and turned back around to see Rennick launching himself at me. I barely had time to twist so that he only caught one side of my body, and when we hit the floor, I arched my back to propel myself into the air and back onto my feet.

He grunted as he pushed off the floor, muttering Zagrath curses and advancing on me again.

I readjusted my grip on the blade. "Did you really think it would be so easy?"

"You were never as good as they thought you were," he said through gritted teeth. "Or *you* thought you were."

"We'll see." My eyes scoured his snug clothing, searching for more weapons he'd tucked away. It would be tricky to kill him with only a single blade, although I'd assassinated targets with much less.

He rushed at me, reaching one arm behind his back and revealing a set of metal nunchucks. As he concentrated on flipping them toward me, I reached behind me and grasped a railing, hoisting myself high in the air and whipping my legs around his neck, the leather of my kilt slapping my thighs. I came down hard, bringing him with me, but I didn't release my legs, tightening them around his neck as he thrashed.

Rennick struck out with the nunchucks, hitting my legs hard enough for me to gasp and loosen my grip. He jerked away from me, leaping to his feet and coughing as he backed up. I also scampered to my feet, crouching low in anticipation of his next attack. He'd always been good. Not as good as me, but good enough to stay alive this long. And in the world of imperial politics and murder, that was an accomplishment.

In the distance, heavy footsteps thundered toward us. Part of me hoped it was Bron, and part of me hoped he was far away from the empire's assassin.

"You know there's only one way off this ship for you," I said, spitting out the coppery taste of blood in my mouth. "The Vandar will never let you live. If you kill me, the Raas will tear you apart with his bare hands."

He cocked his head at me. "If I didn't know what a cold-blooded killer you are, I might even think you admired these brutes and this Raas of theirs."

"I know he's more of a warrior than you could ever be."

Rennick let out a hiss of breath. "You don't know me."

The steel walkways shook beneath my feet as raiders thundered closer. "I know you're going to die."

He chuckled low. "Maybe, but taking you with me will be worth it." Running at me again, he lashed out with the nunchucks.

I dove out of the way, but the metal bar slammed across my back. I rolled across the floor, dodging as Rennick brought his weapon down again and again, the sound of metal against metal reverberating loudly. Jumping to my feet, I leaned back against the railing as he squared off against me, his face red and his eyes wild. My body ached where he'd hit me, but I lifted both my legs and punched out, catching him in the chest and sending him staggering back.

I didn't wait for him to recover, striding forward and pivoting before landing a roundhouse kick that sent him flipping backward over the waist-high railing. Rennick's scream pierced the air as he toppled off the walkway, but before I could celebrate, his hand closed over my foot that was closest to the edge.

As he plummeted down, his weight pulled me with him, dragging me to the edge of the metal walkway. Before going all the way over, I grasped a steel bar and held it with one hand while Rennick held tight to my foot.

"Like I said," he panted beneath me, his maniacal smile wide. "I'm not going without you."

I shook my foot, but his hand held my ankle like a vise. A loud rumbling of voices surrounded me, but I couldn't look up. My grip on the bar was slipping. I had to get Rennick off me or I'd fall.

I realized that my other hand still clutched the blade, so I carefully aimed, then threw it at him. My shaky aim hit him, but only in the shoulder. His smile morphed into a grimace, but he didn't let go.

"Nice try, Mantis. Too bad you're out of options."

I felt my resolve slipping as my fingers lost their hold on the bar, then Rennick's mouth fell open as an axe blade swung down, severing his arm at the elbow and cutting him loose from me. He screamed as he fell back, his arms cartwheeling and his one stump sending a spray of blood through the air.

I closed my eyes so I wouldn't get splattered and so I wouldn't watch myself fall after him, but a thick hand closed over mine just as I started to drop. I opened my eyes and looked up, seeing Raas Bron holding me.

"You were not out of all your options."

CHAPTER TWENTY-THREE

Bron

"I don't understand, Raas," Svar said as we rushed onto the raiding ship. "How could us leading a raiding party onto a lone imperial cruiser put our horde ships in danger?"

I couldn't explain to him that it wasn't so much the horde I feared for as the female in my quarters. I'd honed my instincts over a lifetime of raiding and serving as *majak*, and they were telling me that something wasn't right.

"Where is the other ship?" I asked when I saw that only one of our black beaked ships sat in the hangar bay.

Our pilot swiveled in his chair. "They left with the technology and weapons, Raas."

"At your orders," Svar reminded me.

I pressed my lips together and nodded. "Get us out of here."

"You are sure about leaving the bridge crew alive?" My *majak* asked as the ramp slammed shut and the engines roared to life.

"The captain who'd only been promoted for this job?" I ground my teeth together as I thought about the imperial military commanders who'd chosen the inexperienced crew for us to easily defeat and the clueless captain and pilot to sacrifice to our unknowing wrath. "They are nothing but pawns of the empire." I clenched my hands into fists, thinking of the way the Zagrath had used Alana. "More pawns."

Svar did not speak again as we rocketed off the imperial ship and toward our invisible horde ships, detectable only with our specialized sensors. Even though all of my raiders wore the marks of a successful raiding mission—chests streaked with blood and axes dripping with the evidence of our dominance— the ship was not filled with the chants of victory. We stood with our hands gripping the iron bars above us, but our faces were grim.

This victory was hollow. We'd killed imperial soldiers, but I suspected they'd been fresh out of training. None of them had showed any battle experience. The kills had been easy and without challenge, and now I was almost sure the entire thing had been a ruse and the Zagrath crew sacrificed for a greater imperial purpose. But what was it exactly?

The empire was always trying to eliminate us, just as we were fighting to rid the skies of them. But how would this botched raid do that?

I was running through options in my head when we entered my warbird and touched down, but nothing I could come up with made any sense. I followed my warriors down the ramp, my eyes flicking to the other raiding ships that had arrived before us. Was it the technology we'd taken? Could that have been tracked somehow?

I strode over the ship. The ramp was down, but the engine still hummed. I poked my head inside and my stomach clenched. The pilot was slumped over his console, blood pooling on the smooth surface.

Straightening, I turned to Svar. "There is a Zagrath onboard."

He flinched, his gaze darting to the side. "Should I sound a red alert, Raas?"

I shook my head. "I do not want the enemy to know we are aware of his presence just yet." I locked eyes with each of the warriors from the raiding party. "Fan out throughout the ship and find the intruder."

"Do you want them dead or alive, Raas?" One of the raiders asked.

"I want them stopped."

Low growls accompanied snaps of heels as they rushed off to hunt down the enemy.

I turned to Svar. "You're with me. If the empire sent a solider onto my ship, they might be after the female."

He didn't ask why the powerful Zagrath empire would concern itself with a single escaped miner, but he was a shrewd Vandar. If the empire had gone to such great lengths for the female, it would be hard to convince him she was who she claimed to me.

I didn't have time to think about that as we ran through the ship, racing up swirling staircases and down rattling walkways. Above us, the other warriors from our mission were moving just as quickly through other passageways. The sound of our search echoed within the metal maze.

But another sound made my steps falter. A female scream. *Tvek*.

We were only a few levels away from my quarters, and I pumped my arms by my sides as I ran faster. I leapt from one suspended walkway to another, the hard landing jolting my knees. Svar was close on my heels, the impact of his jump making the floor rattle just as mine had.

I peered up through the dimness. Even though the warriors moving through the ship sent shadows dancing, I could make out Alana. She was facing off with someone dressed all in black—someone who flicked a weapon as he advanced on her.

Jumping from a walkway to a staircase landing, I tracked the battle between the two. Alana was fast, but so was the male she was battling. When she jumped into the air and spun, landing a kick in his chest that sent him flying over the railing, I wanted to cheer. Then just as quickly, she was jerked down, and her hands were scrabbling for purchase as she was pulled over the side.

Svar and I raced up the last staircase as Alana threw a blade that lodged in her attacker's shoulder. Amazingly, he didn't let go, and I saw that her grip on the bar was slipping.

"Nice try, Mantis. Too bad you're out of options," the male hanging onto Alana's foot said, as her fingers uncurled.

Without saying a word, Svar slashed at the male, cutting off his arm while I grabbed Alana's hand moments before she dropped.

She peered up at me in near disbelief as I clutched her small hand in mine.

I swallowed the emotion that thickened my throat. "You were not out of all your options."

Pulling her up, I wrapped my arms around her. "Are you hurt?"

"Nothing that won't heal." She held my gaze. "Thanks for saving me." Then her eyes slid to Svar, who stood next to me, his bloody axe by his side. "You, too."

Svar gave her a silent nod, then addressed me. "Your orders, Raas?"

"Send warriors to find the intruder's body and make sure he's dead." I cut my gaze to the dark depths the imperial fighter had plunged into. "You have the command deck until I join you there. I need to ensure that Alana is not injured."

He tapped his heels in salute, turning and striding off.

I swept Alana into my arms and walked toward my quarters. "Or should I call you Mantis?"

CHAPTER TWENTY-FOUR

Alana

My back throbbed, and my ankle ached as Bron lifted me out of the bathing pools in his quarters. Even though it had been a brief dunk, the hot water had washed all the blood off both of us, and then Bron stood over the powerful drying vents as air blasted away the last traces of water. After he wrapped swaths of fabric around both of us, he set me down on a chair facing the fire. It was only then that I allowed a wave of relief to rush over me that Bron and I were both alive.

"You are sure he didn't wound you?"

"Just bumps and bruises." I flinched as I rearranged the fabric around my chest. At least I wasn't gushing blood, or lying splattered in the bowels of the Vandar ship.

Raas Bron crossed his arms as he watched me. "You want to tell me who that was?"

I thought of Rennick and tasted bile in the back of my throat. "An imperial assassin sent to finish the job I hadn't—and to punish me for my failure, although I suspect he was doing that part for his own enjoyment."

The Raas' expression darkened. "My ship seems to be overrun by imperial assassins."

"He snuck on when your raiding ship returned from the mission. Probably in a small cargo hold or storage unit on the transport. It's a trick I made famous." I cringed when I saw him glowering at me. "Sorry."

Scraping a hand roughly through his unkempt hair, Bron grunted. "It's not your fault. I was too eager to raid the imperial ship. I should have known it was a trap." He took long steps to stand in front of the snapping blue flames. "By the time I realized the crew on the Zagrath ship was all wrong, the first raiding ship had already returned to the warbird—apparently with a stowaway."

I told you keeping me would bring trouble."

He shot a look over his shoulder. "And dropping you off somewhere would keep you safe?"

"No," I admitted, "but it would keep you and your crew safe."

The Raas whirled around, his broad body blocking the light from the fire and casting him in shadow. "Why did you do it?"

I couldn't see his face clearly, but the tremble in his voice gave him away. "Do what?"

"Choose not to carry out your mission. You could have saved yourself a lot of trouble by doing what you've always done."

I flinched at the truth of his words. Killing people *was* what I'd always done. But I hadn't been able to kill him. "I told you. I only kill bad people."

He snorted out a mirthless laugh. "I doubt that is true."

It *was* true, but only partly. I couldn't kill Bron because I recognized a kindred spirit in him—the warrior who'd lost his parents and embraced the horde and his fellow raiders as his only family. I saw in him the same lonely child I had been long ago. Maybe it was that kinship that made my pulse flutter at his touch, or maybe it was something more, something deeper and more primal. Whatever the reason, killing him was impossible. Even thinking of him not being alive made my chest contract painfully.

"All you need to know is that I decided not to kill you," I said. "You and your horde are in no danger from me anymore."

He spun back to the fire, stretching his arms wide and bracing them against the obsidian stone, the fabric around his waist slipping low. "But you remain in danger from the empire."

"Which is why you should drop me off somewhere. I'll only continue to draw imperial wrath."

Raas Bron chuckled, the low sound echoing off the wall. "If you think a Raas of the Vandar would ever run scared from the Zagrath, you have not been paying attention to the ghost stories they tell about us." He glanced at me over one shoulder. "And if you think I would abandon a female I pledged to protect, you have not been paying attention to me."

"Are all Vandar so stubborn?"

He turned, closing the distance between us in two strides and towering over me. "When it comes to our mates, yes."

I opened my mouth to argue again, but he grabbed me by the shoulders and lifted me to my feet.

"I have claimed you by my words and given you the protection of my horde." His body heat pulsed into me as his bare chest brushed my cheek. "But my warriors must believe that you are mine, especially Corvak."

My breathing was shallow as I tipped my head up to meet his molten gaze. His voice had become silken as his whispered words caressed my skin. "He will not be swayed by words alone. He will know if my claims are hollow or if I've fucked you well."

A tremor skated down my spine, sending heat curling in my belly and twitching between my legs. I shouldn't want this. I shouldn't want him. But I did, and more desperately than I'd ever desired anything.

He lowered his mouth, barely feathering his lips across mine. "But I will not take you against your will. You must want this, too."

A jolt went through me, sending frissons of pleasure dancing across my bare flesh. I leaned into his embrace. "I…I…I want…."

What did I want? At the moment, I wanted the muscular alien warrior to keep touching me so that the raging desire storming through me would be quenched.

He gathered both my hands in one of his large ones, his other hand roaming up my body until he tangled his fingers in my hair and tilted my head back. The furry tip of his tail moved up the inside of my thigh, tickling the sensitive flesh there. "Tell me."

Surges of pleasure coursed through me as his breath mingled with mine. My head swam, and my mind was almost as muddled as it had been the night before. "Tell you what?"

He shifted his weight and pressed my body so that I could feel his hardness against the swell of my belly even as his tail flicked between my legs. "Tell me to fuck you and make you mine."

Shivers rolled through me, desire nearly making me whimper. I'd never felt such raw hunger before or the white-hot heat that gathered in my core and made a whimper escape my lips. As the last remnants of control dropped away, I jerked one hand free and hooked it around his neck. "Fuck me, Raas."

With a velvet stare that almost made my eyes roll back in my head, he hitched my legs around his waist and strode across the bedroom until he reached the long dining table. He sat me on the end and dropped down, hooking my knees over his shoulders.

I gripped his bare shoulders, my fingernails cutting into his flesh. "Raas?"

His eyes were half-lidded with desire as he looked up at me. "I will fuck you soon enough. First, I want to taste what is mine."

I fell back with my elbows on the table as he pushed up the fabric wrapped around me and spread my legs, his hot tongue parting my folds. I moaned as he licked me, slowly at first and then his tongue swirled faster when he reached my clit. Lifting my head to watch him drew another strangled gasp from my throat. The sight of his dark head between my legs was almost more than I could take, and I threaded my fingers in his hair as the low simmer ignited in my belly.

My hips twitched as he sucked me, my breath escaping in jagged gasps. I rocked into him, even though I knew I should not be letting myself go so completely. I couldn't stop, and I couldn't hold back, the tremors wracking my body as I detonated. I threw my head back, my hands holding him to me as I jerked and writhed. When his thick finger slid inside me, my body clenched hard around him, and I reared up with a scream.

I collapsed onto the table panting, as he kissed his way up my stomach, tearing aside the fabric and stopping to suck each of my hard nipples as I made soft noises of desperation. I could hardly move, much less speak, and my body prickled with anticipation. Even with my eyes closed, I could hear him tugging off the fabric circling his waist and it hitting the floor.

"Raas," I whispered, my eyes fluttering as I struggled to steady my breath.

He slipped his arms under my back and lifted it off the table, so I was sitting with my ass on the edge and my legs still spread around him. He notched his cock at my slick entrance, and I looked down as he pushed his broad crown inside me. Black swirls like the ones on his chest curled around his thick cock.

I caught my breath as he stretched me, my hands bracing on his chest.

He paused, holding himself partly inside me as he locked his gaze on mine. He cupped my face in one hand, dragging his thumb across my bottom lip. "Call me Bron."

Then his mouth crashed to mine as he drove himself deep.

CHAPTER TWENTY-FIVE

Bron

I thrust hard, the squeeze of her tight heat nearly blinding me with desire. It had been too long since I'd been with a female, but even the pleasurers did not feel as intoxicating as this. I filled her to the hilt, holding myself while she caught her breath.

She moaned into my mouth, her tongue swirling around mine as she curled her arms up under mine and jerked herself closer to me. The human might be small, but her warmth stretched perfectly around me. Pressing my eyes shut for a moment, I savored the tight squeeze of her and the sweet taste of her mouth as she responded eagerly to my kisses.

I'd never been with a human, and I hadn't expected their small bodies to be so adept at giving pleasure. Tearing my mouth from hers, I heaved in a breath as her brown eyes widened, and her mouth opened. My mind drifted to the sight of her battling the imperial assassin and the feeling of clutching her hand before she fell. What had started as a way to protect her and my people had become much more. She was mine to protect and mine to possess. A rumble escaped my throat as I rocked my hips to fill her completely.

"Bron," she whispered.

Hearing my name on her lips sent a thrill through me. I drew myself out and thrust deeper, the need to claim the female storming through me like a fever. I fisted a hand in her hair and held it tight. "Mine will be the last name you cry out."

Her response was to bite her bottom lip and emit a breathy moan, her soft sounds driving me even wilder. I slid my hand down, pressing the flat palm to the small of her back, holding her to me as I moved thickly between her thighs. Every thrust claimed her as mine. Every moan was for me alone.

I looked down to where our bodies met, flesh slapping against flesh, and my cock plunging into her again and again as I claimed her. Unlike the pleasurers I'd enjoyed in the past, I would never share her. Alana was mine.

"You like watching yourself fuck me?" she purred.

I growled and dragged my cock out until only the crown was inside her. I locked my eyes on hers. "I did not think you could take all of me."

She arched her back, her own gaze dropping to watch me slowly thrust myself deep. "I love taking every bit of that thick cock, Raas."

My body jerked at her words, and I rolled my head to one side and tried to hold onto my last shred of self-control. "Alana," I said through gritted teeth, the word both a warning and a caress.

"Raas Bron," she whispered, pulling my head down so that her lips buzzed my ear. "Your cock was made for me."

I jerked at her whispered words. Stifling a roar that was building in my chest, my hips moved quickly as my control shattered. I drove into her again and again, her rapid breaths spurring me on.

She was mine. Her perfect body was mine. No one else would touch her. No one else would fuck her. Mine. My mate.

A growl escaped my lips, and I drowned it by crushing my mouth to hers. Her lips parted willingly, and she let me in with a breathy gasp. The sweet taste of her drove me over the edge, and I pounded into her wildly, swallowing her desperate cries.

"Harder, Raas." Her legs tightened around my waist, as they started to tremble.

Even as I hammered hard, giving her what she asked for, her body fluttered around my cock and then clamped down like a vise. Alana arched her back, her hands clawing at my shoulders. I barely felt the scratches. They were nothing compared to the ecstasy of her velvet heat quivering around my cock. Nothing had ever been as intoxicating as Alana coming around me.

She ripped her mouth from mine, letting out a shaky sigh. "Yes, Bron."

Hearing my name on her lips made my thrusts fast and desperate, and I drove into her hard before knifing up and holding myself deep as I roared my release, pulsing hot into her.

Alana sagged in my arms.

My legs trembled, and I braced one hand on the table, the other circling her waist and keeping her from collapsing. We breathed together without speaking until she let out a throaty laugh.

I cocked my head to one side as I looked down at her.

"Sorry," she said, putting a hand to her mouth. "Now I understand the rumors about human women falling for Vandar raiders."

"There have not been many humans, but now I also understand the appeal of your kind." I swept a damp lock of hair from her forehead. "I never imagined such a small creature could…"

She gave me an arch smile. "Handle you?"

I twitched one shoulder. "Humans are much smaller and Vandar males…"

Alana licked her lower lip. "Have really huge cocks."

I cleared my throat. "I was going to say that we have significant sexual appetites."

She put a hand on my sweaty chest, dragging it down to bump across my stomach muscles. "You don't have to threaten me with a good time."

I placed my hand over hers. "Me claiming you was about more than a good time."

She sighed. "If that was about protecting me, then you can protect me as much as you want." She grinned up at me. "And in as many different ways as we can think up."

My slowing heartbeat thumped faster, and my cock—which was still inside her—swelled again, but I attempted to maintain control. I wanted to tell her about the marks, even though I could not know if she would ever wear mine. "Being claimed by a Raas of the Vandar is—"

"Better than I expected," she finished for me, shifting her hips.

A rush of pleasure sent heat simmering in my core again, muddling my thoughts. "Does that mean you would like more?"

She jerked her body hard, rolling me over so I was sitting on the edge of the table and she was straddling me. She raised herself slightly, then came down again, letting out a breath as she held on with one hand gripping my slick shoulder. "I don't know if I'm ever going to get enough of this."

My eyelids fluttered as her snug warmth enveloped my cock. I cupped her bare ass cheeks, lifting her up and down, savoring the sharp gasp as she took me to the hilt.

She might not understand what it meant that I had claimed her body, but I did. Alana was mine, and she was the Vandar's.

My gaze wandered to the soft skin of her chest. As soon as my marks were emblazoned on her, it would be done.

CHAPTER TWENTY-SIX

Alana

"Are you sleeping?"

His deep voice roused me, and I rolled over. Raas Bron lay naked on top of the bed, his muscular arms bent over his head and his head resting in his hands. The furry tip of his tail curled around one leg and lay still. The lights in the room had dimmed, indicating that it was officially the ship's sleep cycle, and the blue glow from the fire cast dancing shadows over the sharp lines of his face.

I'd never been particularly modest, especially since being an assassin had usually meant seducing my victims, but the Vandar had absolutely no hang-ups about being naked. I suspected they only wore their short, leather battle kilts to keep their junk from being cut off in battle. My gaze fell to the warlord's sizable cock, now stretched down his thigh as he rested. Yep. You would not want something that big swinging loose during a battle.

Bron cleared his throat, and I jerked my gaze to his face.

"I'm awake now." I was covered by the silky sheet, but I draped a bare arm across his chest, welcoming the warmth of his flesh.

Waking up with a man I'd fucked wasn't something I did often. Actually, it might have been a first. Usually I was tugging on my clothes and making excuses so I could return to my place, or even go drink in a canteen for the rest of the night. Curling up next to a male—even one who'd just fucked my brains out—wasn't my thing. Either I didn't want to get attached because I was planning to slit their throat, or I couldn't get involved because I'd be moving on soon.

With Raas Bron I didn't have much choice. I was sleeping in his quarters, and there was only one bed. A bed we'd used thoroughly before collapsing beside each other and falling asleep.

"Who's Lokken?" I asked, as I traced a finger along one of the dark swirls that curled toward his collarbone.

He glanced down at me. "Lokken?"

I lifted my head and rested my chin on the hard swell of his chest muscle. "You yelled something about Lokken the last time you came."

Pink tinged his cheeks, making me wonder what secret I'd unearthed.

"Lokken is one of our ancient gods," he said. "The father of all other gods who forged the universe."

I blinked at him. "So, you were basically yelling 'oh, God?'"

"Humans do not name their gods?" His brow wrinkled in obvious confusion. "How do you keep them all straight."

"I can't speak for all humans, but most human religions have just a single god. Not all, but most of the big ones that we practiced after everyone left Earth."

He shook his head. "One god to create all existence? That would be a very tired god."

I laughed. I'd never given much thought to gods or religions. The Zagrath didn't practice any faith, or tolerate it from any of the planets they controlled, and I didn't know what religion was observed on Faaral, or if my family had believed. My faint memories didn't contain much but hazy images and sounds, many from the night I was taken that I didn't want to think about.

"What is wrong?" He asked, lowering one arm and wrapping it around me.

"What?" I shook the thoughts from my mind. "Nothing."

"Your face suddenly looked pained." He pulled me closer. "Are you sore?"

I laughed again. "Yes, I am sore, you huge brute." I slapped his chest. "But I'm okay. I promise. I just thought about a bad memory."

He nodded. "You were making noises in your sleep at one point. You sounded frightened."

Another reason I didn't sleep with the males I bedded. The nightmares had never stopped, and the time at the imperial academy had only added to the torturous memories that haunted my sleep.

"It's nothing," I told him. "I'm fine. I promise."

He eyed me as if he didn't believe me. "You are not thinking about the assassin?"

Actually, I hadn't been. Rennick was not someone I'd miss, or have any regrets about killing—or helping to kill. He'd been the worst kind of imperial agent—one who had no honor. "No. His is not a death I regret."

He slipped his hand under the sheet and settled it on my back. "I've dreamt about past battles before. The ones where we lost raiders are the ones I seem to relive."

I peered up at his face, his expression fierce in the half light. "I have a hard time imagining the Vandar being defeated. Your ships are invisible."

"Even so, we have lost raiders. Imperial blasters do not always miss, and the Zagrath seem to have an endless supply of faceless soldiers."

I returned my gaze to the inky marks on his skin. "I'm very familiar with Zagrath soldiers."

His hand stilled on my back. "Did you work with them?"

I made a derisive noise in the back of my throat. "Those brainless thugs? No. I always worked alone, but it would be hard to avoid the soldiers entirely." I ran my tongue over the side of my mouth that had recently been swollen. "I've had encounters with them."

As if reading my mind, Bron's gaze went to my faded bruises. "You got those from an imperial soldier?"

I hesitated, but then sighed. I'd already confessed as much to him. "That was partially true. I did get injured by the empire. But I let the soldier rough me up, so you'd believe I was a victim."

A dark rumble escaped from his throat. "You do not have to be their victim ever again."

I lay my head on his chest, soothed by the steady rise and fall of his breath and reassured by his earnest words.

Lying in bed with Bron wasn't so bad. Instead of having the urge to flee, I liked being with him. It felt right, even though in my heart of hearts, I knew it couldn't last. As much as he pledged to protect me, there was only so much one person could do against the might and will of the empire. Or even one horde. I'd worked for the Zagrath long enough to know how long and far they could reach. I'd seen the evidence when Rennick had managed to get himself onto an invisible horde.

Even pressed up against the solidness of the Raas, I felt the pull of the empire. They owned me, and nothing would stop them from finding me and either bringing me back, or eliminating me. An involuntary shudder passed through me, and Bron pulled me closer.

"You still fear the empire?" he asked.

"I know them. They are relentless."

"No more relentless than the Vandar."

I smiled at that. "You *are* incredibly stubborn."

The Raas turned so he was lying on his side and facing me. "Do you trust me, Alana?"

My breath caught in my throat. It had been so long since I'd trusted anyone—longer than I could remember—but as I stared into his eyes, I did trust him. As much as I'd been taught never to trust, the Vandar Raas had managed to slip past my considerable defenses and edge his way into my heart.

It didn't make any sense. I barely knew him, and I was supposed to kill him. Instead, I found myself nodding as my throat tightened. Despite everything I'd been told about the Vandar raiders— the sworn enemy of the empire—I believed Raas Bron. He had already saved me once. He wasn't the ruthless monster I'd been told he was, and he would not lie to me or hurt me. I believed that to my core, even though I should have believed the opposite.

I put a hand to the dark scruff of his cheek. "I trust you."

As he shifted closer to me, there was a heavy pounding on the door, followed by a bellowing voice. "Raas, you are needed on the command deck at once."

My stomach clenched. The Zagrath, I thought. They'd come for me. Again.

Bron rolled over, pinning my body beneath his, and kissed me hard, then he cupped my face as tightly as he held my gaze. "I have pledged myself and my horde to protect you. Never forget that."

And then he jumped from bed, threw on his battle kilt, and was gone.

CHAPTER TWENTY-SEVEN

Bron

I burst onto the command deck, not waiting for my raiders to salute me with their heels. "Report!"

Svar spun toward me, his kilt catching air and slapping his thighs. "We've picked up a distress call, Raas."

The tension in my shoulders uncoiled. After the Zagrath had sent —and lost— another assassin, I'd expected it to be an imperial fleet hot on our tail.

"The Valox," Corvak added, his voice humming with barely contained urgency.

"Here?" I turned to my battle chief then back to the view screen. The Valox resistance was a ragtag operation that had been waging war against the empire less successfully than us. Comprised of fighters from various planets and species, they were able to blend in on imperial outposts whereas we could not, and their ships did not have any distinctive markings like Vandar warbirds. But their nondescript ships could not fly unseen as we could, which left them exposed to Zagrath attacks.

"This is not their usual sector," Svar said, as he pivoted back to his standing console, "but it appears that a battle chased them here."

"How long until we reach them?" I drummed my fingers restlessly on the hilt of my axe. It was not often I was in a position to lend assistance to fellow enemies of the empire.

"Approaching now, Raas." Svar's fingers flew across his screen then he snapped his head up. "On screen."

The streaks of light as we raced through space became pinpoints as we slowed to approach a squadron of battered ships. I leapt down from my vantage point overlooking the command deck and walked to the glass, as if I could get closer to the injured ships. "Damage?"

"They've been badly hit," Corvak said. "But life support appears to be functional, and they do have some shield capacity."

I released a breath. "Hail them and offer assistance."

"Should we drop invisibility shielding?" Svar asked.

I gave a sharp shake of my head. "Not yet. We cannot discount the possibility of an imperial trap." I thought about Alana's insistence that the Zagrath would come after her. "I want full scans of the system. If there's anything out there, I need to know about it."

"Yes, Raas." Svar focused on his screen as he transmitted the hail.

I took long steps to join Corvak at his post. "What do you think, battle chief?"

"I see no reason to think it isn't a damaged squad of Valox resistance fighters, Raas." He tilted his head at me. "Do you have reason to believe otherwise?"

"No," I answered quickly. "But Kratos taught us both to be cautious, and always suspect the empire."

Corvak's upper lip quirked. "We both learned that lesson well. We can never let down our guard when it comes to the enemy."

I slid my gaze to the ships on our screen, their gray hulls scorched and pocked by laser fire. "But we should not withhold aid from those who also fight against the Zagrath."

"Our enemy's enemy is our friend."

I clapped a hand on Corvak's bare shoulder. "Well said."

"Raas." My *majak's* voice pulled my attention. "The Valox have responded to our hail and welcome our assistance. One of their ships has a significant hull breach and another has a damaged engine."

"Are repairs already underway?" I asked.

Svar frowned. "The engineer on one of the damaged ships was killed in the battle and there are only a handful of survivors on the other failing ship."

I considered this for a moment. "Is it safe for us to board and assist with repairing the engine, while the ship with the breached hull is evacuated?"

"I believe so, Raas."

I squared my shoulders. "I will join the boarding parties. Tell one of our engineers to join me on the hangar bay."

"You, Raas?" Corvak asked.

I flicked a glance at him. "I wish to see these fighters who also despise the empire."

"I will join you," he said.

I shook my head. "I need you here monitoring long-range sensors for any enemy activity. If you pick up any incoming attack, I need your battle experience to hold them off until the boarding parties have returned."

He met my eyes with a determined glint in his. "It is done."

"Good." I turned on my heel and headed for the door as my *majak* fell in step with me.

"Before you object," he said, holding up a hand as we passed through the arched doors and stepped off the command deck, "it would be a dereliction of duty for me to allow my Raas to go on a raiding mission without me."

"This is no raiding mission," I said, although I did not slow as we both thundered down the walkway, side by side.

"You do not know what we will find on the Valox resistance ships. Or what will transpire. Just because it has been quiet since we left Zendaren, we should not expect the calm to last."

He had a point, and it was Vandar protocol for my *majak* to be by my side during battle. My fingers tingled at the thought of a fight. Though fucking had slaked some of my desire, my heart still raced at the possibility of another imperial attack.

"I'm afraid we will both be disappointed when we find wounded ships and injured resistance fighters."

"Better than imperial fighters on our warbird attempting to kill our passenger," he said.

I forgot that he did not know what I did about Alana, although I suspected he'd heard the assassin call her Mantis before he'd fallen. If he knew that an imperial assassin remained on board, he would not find our situation so dull. "Peace never lasts long. We will find ourselves drawing Zagrath blood soon enough."

We made our way quickly down the iron stairs, and across rattling bridges that crisscrossed the dark, yawning chasm of the warbird. When we entered the hangar bay, a group of raiders waited next to a raiding ship. I spotted one of our engineers, nodding to him as I hurried up the ship's ramp with the rest of the raiders followed me.

"This time, we guard the raiding ship," I said, once the ramp had slammed shut with a bang and the engines had roared to life. "And take no souvenirs with us."

"Yes, Raas," the raiders replied, their massive arms clutching railings overhead as we rocketed across the hangar bay and toward the Valox ships floating in space like hobbled animals. They'd heard by now of the imperial stowaway, and I knew the security breach stirred anger in all of them. That a Zagrath had been able to sneak onto a warbird and attack a passenger—a female passenger—was a black mark we all wanted to redeem.

My mind went briefly to Alana. I'd left her naked and in bed, which was where I hoped she'd be when I returned. Assisting fellow resistance fighters had fired my blood, but I would need more than a visit to a damaged ship to quench my need.

The ship jolted as we locked onto one of the Valox vessels, and my thoughts focused on the task at hand. Help the Valox, then I could return to my bed and the female waiting for me. My pulse quickened as I rushed down the ramp behind my raiders.

CHAPTER TWENTY-EIGHT

Alana

The ship no longer rumbled from flight, and the view out the wide wall of glass was unmoving. I gathered the sheets around me as I sat up, my pulse fluttering. I didn't know why we'd stopped, but at least there was no sound of battle. I would have known if the empire had found us. Still, my stomach tensed as the flames crackled in the hearth. They'd found me once. They would undoubtedly do it again.

Unlike those who felt uneasy when they were thrust into action, I was most unsettled when I wasn't in motion. I preferred to be prepping for a mission, or in the middle of stalking a target. Anything but waiting.

I huffed out a breath, letting the silky fabric slip to the floor as I stood. Bron had not been gone long, but impatience gnawed at me. Since when did I wait around for someone? Anyone?

I opened the flat-paneled wardrobe built into the ebony wall. Below the row of hanging battle kilts, was a series of drawers. I'd been too crazed when I'd dressed before, but now I took the time to look through the garments. In the first two drawers, I only found swaths of thick fabric, still disheveled from me pawing through them earlier, but in the bottom drawer were garments sized for me.

I held up a fabric kilt, eyeing the nubby, brown cloth. It wasn't exactly chic, but at least I wouldn't be swimming in it. I stepped into the short, pleated skirt, then slipped on a brushed-leather vest and buttoned it.

There were no mirrors in the bedroom, so I padded into the bathing chamber to appraise myself. Standing in front of the long counter, I sized up my new look. My hair was choppy and wild, only adding to the warrior vibe the clothes gave me.

"I guess this is what Vandar females look like," I said, twisting to look at myself from all angles. It wasn't bad, and it did make me feel pretty badass. Since I usually wore clothes that helped me blend in, I wasn't used to such a distinct look. All I needed now were Vandar boots that laced up my calves, and leather braces to sheath my arms. That, and an axe.

The door outside the room swished open, and I poked my head out, expecting to see the Raas, and eager to show him my outfit. But it wasn't Bron. It was a young Vandar boy, carrying a tray on his shoulder as his tail swished nervously behind him.

When he spotted me, the tray bobbled, and he nearly dropped it.

"Sorry to startle you," I said, as he righted himself and proceeded to the dining table.

"It's my fault." He lowered the tray to the table and unloaded the domed plates. "I was told the human prisoner would be here. I shouldn't have been startled."

I bristled at the word prisoner, but didn't argue with him. The boy was clearly only doing what he was told, and it was better for the crew to think I was a prisoner than a spy.

"I was told you'd be hungry." His face flushed, and he didn't meet my eyes. It was also obvious what it meant for a female prisoner to be staying in the Raas' quarters. Not that he would have been wrong in assuming I was famished from sex.

"Thanks." My stomach rumbled as the savory scents drifted to me. "Do you know why we stopped?"

The boy's tail twitched faster. "We're providing aid to some Valox ships."

"Valox?" My interest was piqued. The Valox might not be as vicious or as effective as the Vandar, but were still a thorn in the empire's side. The only reason I hadn't been sent to infiltrate one of their rebel squads was their chaotic organization and lack of any command structure. It was hard to cut off the head of the enemy when we couldn't figure out who led it.

"We'll be back on course soon." The Vandar boy bowed as he backed out of the room, his eyes never meeting mine.

I crossed the space quickly. Now that I'd smelled the food, I was ravenous. I lifted one dome and then another, revealing half a dozen steaming dishes, and a basket of bread knots. The food was unfamiliar, but bread I knew. Grabbing a warm knot, I tore into it and moaned at the yeasty flavor.

There were no utensils, but there was a pile of flatbread stacked high on a plate. Using a wedge of bread, I scooped up a mouthful of one of the soupy dishes. The spice instantly made my eyes water, but I swallowed. Definitely not Zagrath food, but I could get used to it.

As soon as I thought that, I frowned. I shouldn't get used to it. I shouldn't get used to any of it. Not the food or the clothes or even the electrifying touch of the Raas. As much he claimed he could protect me, staying on his horde ship was dangerous. Soon enough, the empire would realize that I'd either been captured, killed, or I'd failed in my mission. They'd come after the Vandar, and when they discovered that I was alive and so was Raas Bron, we would both be targets.

"I should go," I whispered even though there was no one in the room to hear me.

The only time to slip out would be when Bron was gone. Once he returned, he wouldn't listen to my arguments, or care that it was a deadly mistake to keep me on his ship. He was as stubborn as I was, which was infuriating.

I didn't want to go, which was a strange sensation for me. Usually I would be itching to leave and get to my next mission, but there would be no next mission, this time. If I didn't kill the Raas and lead the Zagrath to the Vandar horde, my life as an imperial assassin was over.

I mulled this over for a moment. Would I really miss a life spent hiding and running and killing? My fingers twitched as if reaching for a blade. Maybe parts of it. I had been trained for the job since childhood. It wasn't so easy to shake it off. Then again, it also wasn't easy to think about killing Bron.

I closed my eyes and my heart squeezed. Why couldn't I kill him? He was the enemy, wasn't he? He actively worked against the empire, and I worked for them. I'd been bred to hate his kind, and I should have no problem killing him in his sleep.

But I couldn't. He wasn't what they said about him. None of the Vandar were. I'd seen glimpses of the person beneath the armor and battle axe. Raas Bron did not deserve death. Not by my hand.

My eyes flew open. He also didn't deserve to have the empire pursue him doggedly because of me. My presence in his horde and his bed only put him in greater danger. I ignored the hard ball of regret gripping my belly as I glanced around the room. He would be upset to return to his quarters and find me gone, but he would survive. I thought about the intensity of his gaze, and the sharp lines of his handsome face. For some reason even I didn't understand, I needed him to survive.

Once my mind was made up, I hurried to the door. Holding my breath, I pressed a hand to the side panel. "Please open."

When it did, I stood motionless. I peered out into the open air corridor. In his haste to get to the command deck, he hadn't locked it. Or replaced the guard who'd been killed.

As I left the room, I gave one final glance back, my gut clenching at the bed where his body had warmed me. "I am truly sorry, Raas."

Then I turned and hurried away, running on the balls of my bare feet to make as little noise as possible. The ship was quiet with few raiders moving around, so it didn't take me long to find my way to the hangar bay. I no longer cared about finding a way to send a message to the empire or activate any type of beacon. All I wanted to do was get off the ship and far enough away that I wouldn't draw the empire's attention. Maybe I'd even leave some clues to confuse my superiors and send them spinning in a different direction—one far away from the Raas who'd pledged to defend me.

My heartbeat quickened as I entered the wide-open space of the hangar bay, exposed piping rising high overhead, and the mouth at the far end humming with the energy forcefield. I quickly scanned the black-hulled ships, picking a small one that should be easy to maneuver and making a beeline for it. I needed something fast and small, so I could escape undetected and then drop cosmic breadcrumbs for the Zagrath to follow—away from the Vandar and Raas Bron.

I was so caught up in my plan to that I didn't hear the footsteps until they were practically on top of me. Whirling around, I kicked out, but the raider easily dodged my blow, spinning me around and clamping a thick arm across my throat. Stars danced in front of my eyes as the battle chief squeezed, making it hard for me to draw in air.

"Now why would the Raas' captive—an untrained miner and a victim of the empire—be sneaking onto the hangar bay?" The raider's breath was hot and heavy on my neck as he held me in his punishing grip. "Don't worry, female. I have a feeling you're going to tell me everything once you and I are talking in my *oblek*."

CHAPTER TWENTY-NINE

Bron

"A success, Raas," Svar said as we descended from the raiding ship with the other warriors.

I nodded, although I was not filled with the same exhilaration that a battle or raiding mission provided. I cast my gaze at the raiders' chests, unmarked with the grime of battle and axe blades devoid of blood. None of us were.

My tail twitched in unfulfilled anticipation. "I am glad we were able to provide aid to fellow rebels, but I almost long for the Zagrath to invade an unarmed planet so we will have an excuse to attack."

The Valox resistance ships had been repaired, and their crews redistributed to the strongest ships. Our engineer had even added upgrades to their engines, to aid in their ability to escape quickly from imperial attack.

Svar laughed as we strode across the hangar bay. "Our success at damaging the Zagrath fleet does have disadvantages. We continue to make the enemy weaker, so we will eventually be fighting a foe that is so weak there is no challenge."

"And that will make us weak," I growled.

"There is a universe beyond our sectors and the Zagrath empire. Maybe we search for another foe."

I clapped a hand on his shoulder. "Once we have wiped the empire from existence, then we roam the skies for other sectors to liberate."

Alana would like that, I thought, imagining her by my side as we roamed the galaxy looking for invaders to punish.

Svar gave me a half grin. "I look forward to it, Raas."

"But first, I need to check on my…on the female." I'd almost called her my mate. My pulse quickened at the thought of the word. Alana was not technically my mate, and I hadn't dared to utter the word Raisa, but in my mind, it was done.

Svar nodded, as we walked side by side through the hangar bay doors and began to wind our way up. "You are certain about this, Raas? About keeping the human?"

"Why wouldn't I want to keep her for my pleasure? Raas Kratos took his female as his war prize. Why should I not have the same to warm my bed?"

"Your change of heart was sudden, Raas. That is all."

I snapped my head to him, remembering the buzz among the crew after Kratos had taken his female and brought her on board. Before his decision, no female—and certainly not a human one—had ever flown with a Vandar horde. "Does the crew talk?"

Svar hesitated. "The raiders are curious. After Kratos, they suspect these human females might be bewitching their leaders."

It was said partly in jest, but partly not.

I fisted my hands by my side. If my raiders thought I was being controlled by a female, their faith in me might slip. And a Raas of the Vandar must have the complete faith of his crew to lead them into deadly battles. Hesitation or doubt was the death knell for a Raas and a horde.

"I assure you the female is nothing more than a warm body to sheath my cock—and an eager one, at that." I forced myself to laugh. "Would my raiders deny me release and pleasure?"

"Of course not, Raas."

"Our last visit to a pleasure planet was cut short." I jogged up a twisting staircase. "Maybe if my crew had their own females to entertain them, they would not be so bothered by mine."

Svar let out a low rumble. "You will not get an argument from me, Raas."

We both paused when we reached the doorway to my quarters, and I turned to my *majak*. "I trust you can find a suitable pleasure planet? One that does not entertain imperial soldiers."

I pressed a hand to my door panel, and it slid open. The scent of food welcomed me, and I spotted the plates of food arranged on the table, the domes removed.

Good. I'd ordered food to be sent up so Alana would not get hungry while she waited for me. Then my gaze went to the empty bed.

"I will leave you to your meal," Svar said, the smell of the spicy stews no doubt reaching him, as well.

The back of my neck prickled as I focused on the half-eaten bread knot lying on the floor next to one of the chunky table legs. "Wait." There was no noise from the bathing chamber—not even of arms sluicing through the water—and the soft crackle of the flames echoed ominously off the hard surfaces.

I walked briskly toward the bathing chamber, my gaze taking in the empty room and the placid surfaces of the water in the pools. My stomach plummeted as the truth hit me. Alana was gone.

Running back to where Svar stood in the doorway, his brow creased in worry, I clutched his arm. "She is gone. Did any ships leave while we were with the Valox?"

Svar shook his head. "If any vessels had left without authorization we would have been contacted, Raas."

I let out a breath. "Then she is still on the ship."

My *majak* cocked his head at me. "Why would a female who was running from the empire want to escape our protection, Raas? Especially after we saved her from the imperial intruder." His gaze fell. "Was she unhappy with your arrangement?"

I clenched my teeth, biting back the anger that he would think I would have forced myself on a female who did not want me. "I gave her nothing she did not want."

"Of course, Raas."

I released my grip on Svar's arm. It was not his fault. He did not know the truth about Alana, or why she might feel she needed to get off my ship. I was at fault for keeping secrets from my most trusted advisor. If he harbored any suspicions about Alana, he had not voiced them to me. His loyalty and his trust were absolute, which made me feel even worse, even though the secrets I kept were only to keep Alana safe.

"We need to find her," I said, nodding at a pair of raiders as they passed and clicked their heels in salute. "Initiate a ship-wide search and bring her to me when she is located."

One of the passing raiders stopped and turned. "You do not know, Raas? You have not heard where she was taken?"

Svar and I both pivoted to face him, even as the young raider squared his shoulders as if to brace himself from our penetrating stares.

"Tell me," I said, my words low and dark as I already suspected what his answer would be.

"The female we saved is in the *oblek* with our battle chief, Raas. He caught her on the hangar deck."

The raider bowed his head, but I was already running madly down the walkway, my heart pounding and my eyes red with rage. Svar's rapid footsteps were right behind mine, but I suspected he chased me not because he feared for Alana. He knew to fear for Corvak.

If my battle chief had harmed my mate, I would tear him to pieces with my bare hands.

CHAPTER THIRTY

Alana

"I don't know what you're talking about." I spat out the words even as my voice trembled.

Corvak had strapped me to the wall, although my arms were tied to my sides instead of over my head. At least I wasn't suspended from the chains that dangled down from the ceiling.

There wasn't much to the dark room attached to one side of the command deck. Even though the Vandar warbird was dimly lit in general, this room—the *oblek*, as Corvak called it—had almost no light. There was only the faintest ambient glow from the recessed ceiling above, and the distant points of light out the wall of glass.

My eyes had adjusted to the dark, and I could see the glint of weapons attached to the walls—curved axe blades, pointy daggers, and a spiked mace. So far, the scarred raider hadn't used any of them on me, but I sensed the only reason he hesitated was because I was a female and I'd been favored by the Raas.

"You were attempting to escape," he repeated. "Tell me why."

"I wasn't trying to escape. I was lost."

His laugh was harsh and guttural. "You were being held in the Raas' quarters as his claimed captive. How did you end up in our hangar bay? You have already been attacked by an imperial intruder once. Why would you endanger yourself by leaving the protection of the Raas' quarters?"

I'd been right about the Vandar. They might be huge and ripped, but they weren't brainless brutes. I only hoped this one was as easily manipulated by feminine charms as most males.

Blinking up at him, I let out a breathy sigh. "I told you. The Raas left, and I got bored. The door was open, so I decided to explore. Is that so hard to believe?"

Corvak narrowed his eyes at me. "I was with the Raas when he found you in the battle ring. I saw you move. You are no untrained female who's toiled away in the mines. The Raas saw it, and I see it too." He leaned close, his gaze boring into me. "The real question is why the Raas decided to keep you as a captive, and not rid himself and the horde of you. A female—a human female—is nothing more than a liability for a Vandar horde. Raas Bron knows this. He saw it for himself with Kratos." He spun on his heel and took long steps toward the glass, clearly talking to himself and not me anymore. "He should have known the dangers of keeping you, but still he did it." He swiveled back to face me. "Then an imperial attacker sneaks onboard our warbird and tries to kill you. Why?" His dark pupils flared with curiosity. "Who are you?"

"I've told you who I am."

Corvak's lip curled up as he advanced on me. "You've peddled lies to the Raas, and now you're trying to sell them to me. I have no interest in whatever magic between your legs you've used to bewitch him. Tell me the truth, and I'll release you."

The doors swished open, muffling his final words.

"You'll release her now." Bron stood silhouetted in the arched doorway, his legs wide and one hand gripping the hilt of his axe.

Corvak straightened. "You are back, Raas."

Bron walked into the room with his *majak* behind him. His glance at me was brief, but he positioned himself between me and his battle chief. "And I find that you've taken my female from my quarters."

Even I cringed at the deadly menace in the Raas' voice. His rage simmered just below the surface, making his voice vibrate.

"I did not take her from your quarters, Raas." Corvak braced his feet wide as he faced Bron. "I discovered her in the hangar bay, attempting to escape."

The Raas flinched almost imperceptibly, but he did not turn to look at me.

"I tried to explain that I was lost," I said, but Bron held up a fist to silence me.

Shit. He was almost as furious at me as he was at his battle chief. If I wasn't certain Corvak would torture me, I might have opted not to be saved by the enraged Raas.

"If she was lost, you should have returned her to my quarters." Bron's gaze was fixed on Corvak.

"And if she was not lost, Raas?" he answered, sharply. "If she is not who she claims to be and is a danger to you and to this horde?"

"That is for me to determine as Raas. Not you!" Bron's voice rose to a shout, the sound bouncing off the hard walls and reverberating through my bones.

"And if you are unable to see the truth?" Corvak yelled back. "If you have been blinded by the temptations of the flesh and have chosen the human over your horde?"

Svar sucked in a breath, his own hand going to his weapon. "Stand down, Corvak."

The Raas and his battle chief stood across from each other, faces red and chests heaving.

"I cannot," Corvak said, drawing his axe.

"You would defy your Raas?" Svar asked, his voice a hiss.

"My duty is to the Vandar and the horde above all else." Corvak flicked a derisive glance to me. "As battle chief, I must fight against all threats—even ones who spread their legs to get special treatment."

Bron drew his axe so quickly, I flinched. "If you dishonor her, you dishonor me—and the horde."

"She is nothing but a human female," Corvak tossed his axe from one hand to the other. "A female who is lying to you."

Bron assumed a low battle crouch. "She has not lied to me. And she is not just a female. She is my mate."

The last words seemed to land on Corvak like physical blows. He jerked back, almost dropping his weapon. "*Tvek*. What spell has she cast over you?"

"No spell. I have claimed her, as is my right as Raas." Bron circled his battle chief, eyes blazing.

"Did you not see what happened to Kratos?" Corvak moved in the opposite direction. "Do you wish our horde to be ripped apart once more?"

"It is you who is threatening the horde." Bron lunged at Corvak, slicing his blade through the air. "With your treason!"

I gasped as Corvak spun away, dodging the attack and lashing out himself. He swung his axe up, forcing Bron to leap to one side.

Svar moved behind the Raas, his face twisted in concern. "This should not be settled here."

"Agreed. We would not be here, if my female had not been brought here against her will and mine." Bron barreled toward Corvak with his axe held high. "Honor must be defended."

"I am defending honor." Corvak grunted as he dodged the attack and stumbled away, hitting the glass wall. He swiveled and struck Bron in the back with the flat of his blade. "The honor of the horde."

Bron staggered away, the hit obviously startling him.

This was not good. If Corvak won, I was going to be tortured and put out an airlock, for sure. If Bron won, I would have a lot of explaining to do. He knew as well as his battle chief did that I had not gotten lost and ended up on the hangar bay. He knew the truth, even if he couldn't admit it.

"Stop!" I yelled, over the heavy breathing and angry grunts.

Neither Vandar paid any attention to me. Even Bron cut his eyes to me, and the hardness in them made fear ice my veins.

With a deafening roar, the Raas leapt through the air, his axe coming down hard on Corvak's. The battle chief's weapon clattered to the floor, and Bron kicked it away, looming over his opponent with his own axe poised to strike.

Corvak did not look away. Instead, he glared at his Raas. "Do what you must. I die with no regrets."

The Raas' chest rose and fell as he drew in ragged breaths, then he backed away. "I will not kill you."

Svar swung his head to Bron. "Raas—?"

"But you cannot stay as my battle chief, or as part of my horde," Bron continued, locking eyes with his *majak*. "Banish him at the first habitable planet."

Corvak's jaw tightened. "I would prefer death."

"You do not get to choose," Bron said. Without another word, he walked to the wall and unhooked me, his movements rough and jerky.

"Raas," I began, not sure if I should apologize, or thank him, or both.

His cold gaze slid to me. "Unless you wish to be banished alongside my battle chief, it would be best if you did not speak."

Then he threw me over his shoulder and stalked away from his gaping officers and out of the *oblek*. The last thing I saw, as I hung down the Raas' back was the murderous glare from Corvak, before the iron doors slid shut on him.

CHAPTER THIRTY-ONE

Bron

My body burned as I stormed through the ship, the female bouncing against my back. At first, she was quiet, but after I leapt down a few staircases, she slapped her hands against the bare skin of my back.

"You can let me down now. You've made your point."

I stomped down a walkway, the metal trembling beneath my thundering boots as raiders scurried out of my way, their eyes cast down out of respect and fear. "I am not making a point. I am making sure you do not run off again."

She started to argue with me, but I landed a sharp slap on her ass. "I suggest you cease your complaints, unless you want more of that. Make no mistake, female. I have no problem meting out the punishment you so richly deserve."

I reached the door to my quarters, slamming my palm against the panel to open them and walking straight through the sliding steel to drop her onto my bed. She bounced a couple of times, after landing on her back, and then glared up at me.

"What the hell was that all about?" Her face was flushed, no doubt from hanging upside down.

I backed away from the foot of the bed and raked both hands through my hair. "I should ask you the same question. Why did I find you being questioned by my battle chief, when I left you in my bed?"

"You didn't really expect me to lie here waiting for you like some helpless woman, did you?"

"I expected you not to attempt to steal a ship and run away from me," I said, the tremor in my voice betraying the fact that I was attempting to remain calm and having a hard time doing it.

"Then you don't know me very well," she snapped back.

I dropped my hands to my knees and leaned over, breathing unevenly. I'd just battled my own warrior over her and exiled him from my horde, and she was claiming I didn't know her? When I looked up at the female on my bed, her eyes flashing defiance, a wave of defeat washed over me, dousing my fury and quelling the heat in my body.

What did I know of her, aside from the truths she'd finally confessed under the influence of the ancient oils? I knew she ignited my desire and enflamed my body. I knew being buried inside her made me feel like a god. But I did *not* know what truly dwelled in her heart—the heart of an imperial assassin. And I could not understand how deeply the empire had twisted her mind and ingrained loyalty to them, despite abusing her and molding her into a killer.

"You are right. I do not know you." Straightening, I backed away from her, turning and walking toward the bathing pools.

The red haze of rage had cleared from my vision, but my footsteps were still halting as I made my way into the chamber. I leaned my hands against the long counter and sucked in greedy breaths, the cool stone welcome on my scorched skin.

"What have I done?" I said under my breath, too afraid to utter the words any louder. A Vandar Raas did not doubt his actions or second-guess himself, but how could I not? I'd defended a virtual stranger over one of my officers, and cast him out of the horde. My mind whirled as I tried to recall when a raider had last been exiled, and I clenched my teeth to keep the scream from escaping my lips.

I'd had no choice. Corvak had challenged me. Even if I knew Alana was not who she claimed to be, and my battle chief was correct in his doubts, I could not let his challenge remain unanswered. He'd directly threatened my command and authority. No Raas could let that stand.

I thought of Kratos, wishing desperately he were here instead of me. What would I have advised him, if I'd been *majak* and he'd been challenged by Corvak over his female? I choked back a laugh as I thought of the former Raas and my friend. I would not have been able to hold him back from killing Corvak.

Kratos had been wild with terror when he'd thought his female had been taken by attackers, and had shown no mercy to the aliens who'd attempted to harm her. He'd put Corvak in his place when the battle chief had questioned his leadership after taking the female on board. I shook my head. No, Kratos would have done no differently than I had.

I peered up at myself in the reflective surface above the counter. Sweat streaked my face, and my hair was tousled. Then why did I feel like I'd failed as Raas? Why did Corvak's words echo in my head? Why did a part of me believe he was right, and I was making a deadly mistake?

Had he been defending the honor of the horde, while I risked my raiders by keeping Alana onboard? Was I putting my own desires above those of the Vandar? If so, this was a crime from which I could never recover.

I met my own eyes in the mirror, searching for the weakness and treachery my battle chief had claimed to see.

"No," I growled. My gut told me that Alana was no threat. If she was in danger from the empire, then it was my job to keep her safe. If the Zagrath wanted her dead as badly as she said, then keeping her alive and away from their grasp was my most crucial mission. If she was an imperial asset, then keeping her as a Vandar prize would be a blow to the enemy, regardless of my wants.

My mind drifted to the female I'd left on my bed, and I jerked off my belt and let my kilt fall to the floor. I needed to cool off and rid my thoughts of her. Tugging off my boots and armor, I strode to the shower and pressed a series of buttons to activate the overhead waterfall.

As expected, the water was a cold shock to my system as it cascaded down. I braced my arms on the wall and let it hammer at the knots of my shoulders as it warmed. Slowly, my anger subsided, and my heartbeat slowed. Right or wrong, I'd made my decision. It was done, and I would have to live with my choice.

Then I heard her voice behind me, and desire ignited in my core again. The desire to punish her for her betrayal and to cut down anyone who tried to take her from me.

CHAPTER THIRTY-TWO

Alana

I watched him stalk away from me, his hands in fists by his side.

Shit. That hadn't gone like I'd wanted it to. All my intentions to apologize for trying to leave and thank him for defending me had flown out the window the moment I'd felt cornered. He'd done nothing but stand up for me, even when he knew I was in the wrong and his battle chief was right to be suspicious. Now, he'd exiled one of his own raiders, and I was acting like an ungrateful child.

I groaned and climbed off the bed. The least I owed him was an explanation. One that didn't come with snark or complaints.

Loud breathing echoed from the attached room. The guy was clearly pissed. Not that I blamed him, but maybe I should wait until he cooled off.

"That could take the rest of the journey, Alana," I told myself. "Besides, since when are you afraid of a guy's temper?"

If I'd handled the hair-trigger temper of my grappling instructor at the Zagrath academy and his fondness for beating the shit out of me, I could handle the Raas. In my gut, I knew he'd never hurt me. At least, not physically. Like I'd suspected, the Vandar still held to old-fashioned ideas about women. While I didn't buy into their overprotective-caveman crap, I didn't mind the certainty that Bron wouldn't strike me. It was more than I could say for the males I'd known who didn't see any harm in dominating a woman with their fists. Killing them had always been more of a pleasure than a job.

I took tentative steps toward the attached bathroom. Instead of the splash of water from the pools, the sound of rushing water came out of the open doorway. When I reached the arch and peeked my head around, my breath caught in my throat.

Although I'd seen that the glossy black wall at the far end of the room had buttons, I'd never given much thought to it. Not that my thoughts were very focused now as I watched Raas Bron standing under a torrent of water spilling from a narrow ledge overhead. His arms were braced wide as the water pounded his shoulders and his bare back was to me. And what a glorious bare back it was.

My nipples hardened and heat pulsed between my legs as I watched him. Sure, I'd gotten a good look at him earlier in bed, but it had been dark. Now I could really drink in the sight of his muscular legs, firm ass, and broad back that tapered to a narrow waist.

"Fuck me," I murmured, confident that he couldn't hear me over the rushing water.

I forced my gaze away from his naked wet body. You're here to explain yourself, Alana. Not gawp at him like a horny Burglig. I shook aside the thought of the bug-eyed creatures with no eyelids and walked into the room.

"Hey," I called over the noise. "I'm sorry."

Without stopping the flow of water, he turned around.

My mouth went dry. Fuck me. Again.

Without his kilt or shoulder armor or leather forearm guards, I could finally see the massive Vandar completely naked. My gaze shifted from his sculpted chest to his ridged stomach, and finally to the thick cock hanging between his legs, black markings wrapped around the shaft like the ones curling across his chest.

"What?" He swept his hands over his face and blinked at me, water hitting his back and spraying off his body.

I stepped closer, droplets stinging my face. "I said, I'm sorry."

He tilted his head then shook it. "You are what?"

Huffing out an impatient breath that the infuriating alien didn't just turn off the water so he could hear me, I took another few steps to close the distance between us, wiping the spray from my own face as it hit me. "I said, I'm—"

He snaked an arm out and hooked it around my waist, jerking me under the water and then spinning me so that my back was pressed flat to the wall and his body pressed hard to my front to immobilize me.

"What the actual…?" I spluttered, as warm water ran down my face and into my eyes and mouth.

"I should punish you," he said, his voice a throaty rumble that cut through the sound of the water. Even though the water was warm, his naked body was even warmer against me.

My pulse fluttered nervously. Had I been wrong about the Raas?

"Or maybe I should fuck the defiance out of you, instead?"

My breath caught in my throat, and my heart hammered wildly. Even though I was pinned to the wall by his rigid body, I struggled against him. "I said, I'm sorry."

"You're sorry?" His head was next to mine, his mouth against my ear. "Sorry for running from me, or sorry for getting caught? Sorry that you didn't trust me to keep you safe after I saved your life? Or sorry that I was forced to fight over you and exile one of my raiders?"

I pushed against him, but he was too big to budge. "I'm sorry you still don't get why I have to leave."

Not exactly my best apology, but not my worst.

He ground himself into me, his cock now hard. "I told you. You cannot leave."

Arousal coursed through me, but I shook my head. "You have to let me go. If you don't, the empire will come after both of us again. But the next time, it won't be just one person. And they won't stop until they've killed me and you."

"I will stop them." He pulled his face back so he could meet my eyes, even as water cascaded behind him.

I believed that he would try, but I also knew the empire. Too well. I hitched in a breath. "I can't let you risk everything for me. It's too much."

"Because I don't know you?" He cupped my face in one hand.

"You don't. If you knew me, and all the things I've done, you'd be glad to be rid of me." The truth of my words made a knot form in my gut. No one should want someone like me. Not after what the empire had made me.

He tipped my chin up. "You are wrong. If you left, I would never stop searching for you." He brushed a kiss across my lips. "You are mine, now. The good and the bad."

A strangled sob worked its way up my throat. How could he believe that after what I'd done? After what I'd forced him to do? It didn't make any sense.

"I told you that a Vandar Raas never lies. We also never give up." He dragged his thumb across my bottom lip. "Do you think that after battling the empire for millennia, I would be scared by them coming after you?" His eyes were molten, searing his words into me. "Let them come, and I will rain fire on them for daring to threaten my mate."

"You don't want a mate as bad as me."

"I want you," he said. "No matter how bad you are."

In that moment, I believed him. I was his, and he would die to protect me. I opened my mouth to speak but he tangled a hand in my hair, and jerked my mouth to his.

Need stormed through me like fire, scorching everything in its path as I arched into him, deaf to the water rushing around us. All that mattered was the burn of his flesh against mine, and his hot tongue plundering my mouth.

His mouth claimed mine as possessively as his hands that moved roughly down my body until he reached my ass. He lifted me up with a fast jerk, spreading my legs and wrapping them around his waist as the fabric of my kilt rode up and bunched around my stomach. A desperate breath escaped my lips as he pressed me hard against the slick, stone wall, rocking into me.

I didn't just want him to fuck me. I needed him inside me, as if being filled by him would burn off the desire that clawed at me like an untamed beast and kill off the creature the empire had made me into.

"Fuck me, Bron," I said after ripping my mouth from his.

His predatory gaze locked on me, his dark eyes savage as he notched his cock at my entrance. "You could not stop me."

Then he thrust hard and fast, causing all the breath to leave me. I lost the ability to think, my heart hammering as he impaled me against the wall. Bron's jaw was tight as he moved thickly between my legs, my own legs sliding down his wet back as water rushed over them.

I clutched his shoulders, heat rolling through me as he fucked me against the wall. His rhythm was punishing, but I welcomed each deep thrust and the spirals of pleasure making me moan and shake.

"You needed this, didn't you, my bad mate?" he gritted out, the veins in his neck straining. "Needed to be punished."

I could only whimper in response, as he drove into me without mercy. When my body started to tremble, I scraped my fingers through his hair and pulled his eyes to mine. His claiming gaze scoured my face as I lost control and shattered in his arms, gasping his name.

Lodging his cock deep for a moment as I quivered around him and arched my head back, Bron pulled my face back to him. "My bad girl," he husked.

Then he pistoned into me with primal fury, roaring as he exploded inside me. My legs slipped down as he sagged into me, and my body hummed from the pleasure of his exquisite punishment.

CHAPTER THIRTY-THREE

Bron

"*Vaes!*" I didn't turn as the doors to my strategy room opened, but I knew it was Svar, and what he'd come to report.

A quick tap of his heels told me he was standing at attention behind me. "It is done, Raas."

I stood at the wall of glass, my gaze fixed on the burnished, brown surface of the planet below us. Kimithion III was a class-M planet, with a pre-warp society that had so far avoided war, famine, and imperial rule. It was also the new home of my former battle chief.

I nodded but remained facing the glass. I did not want to see the disapproval on my *majak's* face. "You do not agree with my decision."

He hesitated before releasing a long-held breath. "He gave you no choice."

"But you would have made a different one?" I pivoted to face him. "If I was still *majak*, I would also doubt such an extreme action."

Even Kratos with his dark impulses never exiled a raider, I thought, before pushing the doubt aside.

"The planet is acceptable, and the people do not have any issue with him living among them," Svar reported, his voice devoid of emotion.

"The residents of the planet are…?"

Svar glanced down at the tablet in his hand. "A mixture of humans and native Kimithions. The natives maintain governmental rule, but the humans appear to live side by side with them and sit on their counsel, although they are not compatible for mating with each other."

I cocked an eyebrow.

"The Kimithions are cold-blooded creatures with scales for skin and an entirely different reproductive system than humans."

"As long as they can manage to keep the Zagrath at bay," I said, knowing that Corvak could not endure imperial rule, nor would I be so cruel as to force that upon any raider, no matter their crime.

"I'm afraid there is little of value for the empire to take." Svar tapped his screen. "Aside from an arid climate that appeals to the cold-blooded natives, it is a barren place."

I swallowed down the bitter taste of regret. If I could undo my actions, I would, but going back on a pronouncement of exile would be admitting weakness. If I did that, I might as well surrender my horde. Weakness was not something a Raas could indulge. Nor was a challenge as bold as the one Corvak had made.

My *majak* lowered his device. "He will be safe—if restless—until…"

"You've already sent word to the other hordes?"

He inclined his head. "On an encrypted channel, as you requested."

I pressed my lips together, spinning back around. "Good. He will not go unclaimed for long. He is a tough fighter."

Although it had not been done in a generation or two, a Vandar raider could move between hordes. Joining a horde was almost always for life, but there were cases of warriors moving from one to another. I doubted that Raas Toraan would have the stomach for such an impulsive battle chief as Corvak, but Raas Kaalek might appreciate the raider's thirst for battle and impatience to spill blood. Kaalek had always been the least disciplined of the brothers.

Then there was always the fourth Raas. The one who patrolled the hinterlands and was not related to the three Raas brothers. Would the mysterious Raas Vassim trek across sectors to retrieve an exiled raider?

No one had seen him or his horde since he wrested control from the deranged Raas before him. He'd pledged to restore balance to his horde and cease the violence that had earned their reputation as monsters who feasted upon flesh and torched everything in their path. Rumors drifted across space from the far reaches where Raas Vassim wandered—whispers of debauchery so wild that even the empire had avoided contact—but little was known if these were spread by the Zagrath, or the Raas himself.

"Our transmissions have been received by all and acknowledged by all but one," Svar said.

He did not need to tell me which one. "Corvak might do well with the unknown Raas. If his horde still flies."

"We would have heard if it had been destroyed. Even so far away, word would have reached us of such a defeat."

Svar seemed sure, but I was not. It wasn't that I believed Raas Vassim would be bested by imperial forces. My concern was that he'd gone rogue and no longer patrolled the ominous space beyond the more populated sectors.

His predecessor had gone insane flying through the emptiness that was the hinterlands. Who was to say the same fate had not befallen Raas Vassim? It had been so long since he and his horde had been heard from that they were not even mentioned on Zendaren. Even the old Raas Maassen who seemed to know all just shook his head and glowered at the mention of the fourth horde.

"Then let us hope the fourth horde comes for Corvak," I said, taking a deep breath. "The wildness of uncharted space may suit him."

Svar nodded, but he looked as unsure as I felt.

I rested one hand on the hilt of my axe. "We should depart and resume our course."

"Yes, Raas. Do you still wish to make a stop—?"

"On a pleasure planet?" I allowed myself a small smile. "Yes. Our raiders need it more than ever, now."

The corners of Svar's mouth twitched and relief passed over his usually solemn face. "Agreed, Raas. I've already plotted a course. We should arrive at Laurinia by first watch."

"Laurinia?"

"We have never visited this particular planet. It is new, but they are already known for their variety and unique environment."

"Environment?"

"The Laurinians have spent considerable coin to make their city into a hedonistic playground." Svar's smile widened. "Our raiders will be pleasantly surprised."

Most of the pleasure planets we frequented were weathered and tended toward seedy. A hedonistic playground—whatever that was—would be a welcome change.

I swiveled back to the glass, giving a final look at the planet's surface. "As long as the empire has not also become aware of this playground."

The pleasure planets we'd chosen in the past were also ignored by the Zagrath, and far out of imperial territory.

"From what we know, they have not, but we are enacting strict security protocols. We will not land on the surface, and our horde ships will send raiders in shifts. Shall I notify you in your quarters when we arrive, Raas?"

I thought about the female waiting for me back in my quarters. I might have convinced her that she would be safer on my horde and with me, but as much time as we'd spent in each other's arms over the past few rotations, there was no indication of mating marks on her skin or mine. Her soft, smooth, unmarked flesh tormented me, and served as a stark reminder that as much as I might insist she was mine, the female assassin might never truly be my mate.

She might never belong to anyone.

"Let me know when we arrive. I would like to see this Laurinia for myself." I turned sharply from the view of the planet and tried not to imagine my battle chief watching as his horde—and the only family he'd ever known—flew away.

CHAPTER THIRTY-FOUR

Alana

I sat in front of the fire with my feet tucked up underneath me, staring into the flames. I'd stayed away from the glass since we'd reached the planet, and now that the familiar hum of the engines had resumed, I released a long breath.

As an assassin to the empire, I'd grown used to bringing death with me. It shouldn't bother me that I was the reason Bron had been forced to exile one of his closest officers. It wasn't like the warrior had been executed for his actions. Considering how livid Bron had been when he'd found me strapped to the wall in Corvak's *oblek*, the battle chief might have gotten off easy.

But all the deaths I'd been responsible for had been for people who deserved it. At least that was what I told myself. Even the ones who weren't evil, had no problem being seduced by a total stranger. They got what they deserved, I'd always thought.

Unfaithful, greedy males who'd stood in the way of the empire's expansion throughout the galaxy.

But Corvak was not unfaithful or greedy. He'd only been following his instinct about me.

"An instinct that was right." I shifted and reached for the goblet of Vandar wine beside me.

Even though Bron had forgiven me and assured me that I was not the reason he exiled his battle chief, it was not true. The Raas did lie, after all.

I took a swig of wine, finally glancing over my shoulder at the view as we flew through space. I didn't know where we were going next, but at least we would not be hovering above Kimithion III anymore. Every moment we'd stayed was a moment of torture and a reminder that I was the reason Bron had been forced into an impossible decision—me or his crew mate.

Even now, I had a hard time believing he'd chosen me. No one had ever chosen me above duty or the job. My throat was thick as I thought about the Raas whose bed I was sharing. The Raas I would have to leave, one way or the other.

As much as I wanted to stay, and as easy as it felt when we were together, the hard truth was that an imperial assassin and a Raas of the Vandar could not be together. One day, someone would discover the truth about me, and it would be the end of Bron. He would lose his role as Raas and end up like Corvak, exiled to a strange planet. Or worse, we'd both be executed for treason. That was, if the empire didn't find us both first.

I gulped down a mouthful of wine, letting the tang pucker my cheeks. I knew firsthand that the Zagrath had eyes and ears everywhere. As insular as the Vandar hordes were, they did stop on pleasure planets and make supply runs. One day, word would escape that Raas Bron kept a human female, and then the empire would know.

The wine churned in my stomach. My own death didn't upset me. I'd always known my life would end as I'd lived it—in violence. But Raas Bron did not deserve my fate. Even less did he deserve what would happen if the Vandar discovered he'd knowingly kept an imperial spy and assassin in their midst. His *majak* had been there when Krennick had called me Mantis, although in the chaos he might not have registered the out-of-place word. Still, it was only a matter of time before there were more slips. It was inevitable. As was the fall of Raas Bron, if he kept me.

As the wine sent tingles down my arms and dulled the ache in my chest, I knew what I would have to do. Getting off the ship without being seen or stopped was too difficult, especially now that the Raas kept a guard posted outside his quarters.

No, I'd have to convince him to let me off the ship. Then I could slip away. I chugged the rest of the wine, hating that I had to deceive Bron in order to save him. But he was too honorable to save himself. He'd promised to protect me, and he would do so even if it meant his death or his own exile.

"Well, I'm not going to let that happen," I muttered to myself as I stood. I'd finally met a truly good guy. I wasn't going to let him destroy himself over me.

The door swishing open made me turn, forcing myself to smile as the Raas entered the room. His stormy expression softened when he saw me. "You waited for me."

I swallowed the bitter taste of regret as I walked toward him, smiling seductively and adding an extra twist to my step. "You thought I wouldn't, Raas?"

His brow furrowed but relaxed when he spotted my empty glass. "Vandar wine?"

I shrugged. Let him think the wine was loosening my inhibitions instead of my cunning. He would not be the first to be taken in by my feminine innocence—at least the appearance of it. I shook off any guilt that I was tricking the Raas. Despite what he promised and what I'd allowed myself to believe in the heat of the moment, I knew the reality of the empire's reach and power. And I was not willing to sacrifice his life to it.

"We've left the planet's orbit and are on course for Laurinia." He unhooked his shoulder armor by the door, hanging it on a stand, and then unlaced his boots.

"Laurinia?" I helped him pull off his leather arm coverings without him asking, letting my hands linger on his warm skin.

"A pleasure planet we've never visited. The crew needs a break. Our last missions have been unrewarding."

I studied his face. "I suspect the Raas also needs a break. Will you be going down to the surface with your raiders?"

His gaze slid to me. "Not to indulge in the offerings, but I will visit to appraise the planet. It is reputed to be an impressive sight."

"Bron." I took his hand and led him to the bed, pushing him down so he was sitting on the foot of it. "You do not need to deprive yourself because of me."

One of his dark eyebrows lifted, as he wrapped his arms around my back. "You think I'm depriving myself when I'm fucking you every night?" He tugged me so that I stood between his legs. "There is nowhere I would rather be than inside you."

Warmth suffused my face, and liquid heat stirred in my belly. "Then why don't we sample the pleasure planet together?"

Raas Bron frowned, even as he lifted my wrist and feathered a warm kiss across the delicate skin. "You want me to take you off the ship?"

The unspoken reason this was such a problematic idea hung in the air between us.

I couldn't sound like I wanted it too badly. The Raas was clever. He would see through me if I pushed too hard. I kept my voice light, twitching one shoulder as if it was of little consequence. "I thought it could be fun, but I don't have to go. I can wait for you here."

He leaned back and looked at me. "You must have been to pleasure planets before. In your previous line of work."

"Only a few seedy ones. If this Laurinia is so special, maybe we could sample the offerings together." I held up a finger. "Without the assistance of any pleasurers."

"You do not wish to share?" he teased.

I crawled on top of him and straddled my legs around his waist. "No." I dragged my palms down the hard slopes of his chest. "I want you all for myself."

A velvet growl rumbled in his throat. "You know you have me, Alana."

I leaned down and nipped his ear. "I haven't had you on Laurinia."

He laughed, coiling an arm around my waist and flipping me onto my back in a single, smooth motion. "Maybe we could arrange an outing to the planet." He hovered over me, his eyes sparking with heat. "As long as you promise not to attempt another escape."

I wrapped my legs around his back, squeezing and crossing my feet briefly at the ankles. "I'll only run from you, Raas, if you insist on a chase."

He reached for my wrists, lifting them over my head and pinning them easily to the bed. "Caught you."

For now, I thought, as his mouth crashed into mine, and I surrendered to him, my heart breaking a little as the traitorous thought whispered in the back of my mind. *For now.*

CHAPTER THIRTY-FIVE

Bron

"You're sure about this?" Alana didn't glance up at me as we stood together on the transport, the ramp touching down on the surface of Laurinia and sending sunlight flooding the compact compartment.

I wasn't sure about my decision, but I was learning to live with uncertainty. Besides, the reports of the pleasure planet and it's exotic environments had been too tempting to ignore, even for one who had no intention of engaging a pleasurer.

"If you can promise me you won't try to steal a ship and escape from me."

She snorted out a laugh as we both peered outside. "Even I'm not crazy enough to run away from this."

I took her hand and walked down the ramp, my own mouth gaping as I took in Laurinia. Our transport ship had landed on a circular pad, but it was surrounded by water. A long walkway connected it to a stretch of pink sand that was lapped by sea-green water so clear it was easy to see vibrantly hued creatures darting within its depths. There were fabric cabanas on the beach, some with sheer fabric walls closed so that only the hazy outline of writhing bodies could be seen and others with pristine white curtains drawn to reveal females reclining on wide, cushioned platforms, their bodies beckoning males to join them. Pod-like boats hovered above the surface of the water, scantily clad pleasurers lounging on pillows while musicians sat on the edges of the boats and played. Everywhere, music and moans rose into the air.

Beyond the sand, gleaming white cliffs towered high with glistening chrome villas jutting out from them like wedged saucers. Even from where we stood, I spotted pools of water attached to the disc-like structures, seemingly suspended in mid-air like teardrops of water. The shiny metal structures had balconies covered by gossamer awnings and held platform beds where naked bodies openly cavorted with each other.

"Are those your warriors?" Alana asked, shading her eyes with one hand as she squinted toward the cliffs.

My raiders had descended to the planet first, each horde ship sending its crew in waves and keeping a small complement on board. Even though Laurinia assured us that she had excellent aerial defenses, we did not take chances with security. I'd waited until Svar had returned from his time on the surface to leave the warbird in his hands, so I could truly indulge without worry.

"I would assume so. We paid the madam handsomely for exclusive access." Although I saw dark hair and broad backs, I didn't look closely. I needed to serve with my raiders after they'd had their fill of females and fun. On other pleasure planets, our activities were usually confined to private chambers. On Laurinia, there seemed to be nothing private. The Vandar were not known for being modest about our bodies, but we also did not regularly fuck in open view of superior officers.

"I don't get it. Aren't Vandar raiders known for pillaging and raping? Why would you ever have to pay for women?"

I bristled at the comment. "Vandar do not rape. That is what the empire wishes you to believe. We pay for services we require, and we only pillage from the empire." I waved a hand at the gleaming city rising up from the pristine beach. "This is not the empire."

"I can see that," Alana muttered. "The Zagrath are way too uptight for this. They'd probably never remove their helmets."

I gave her a side-eye glance. "You have been with many of these helmeted fighters?"

She wrinkled her nose as we walked toward the sand. "Definitely not. Imperial soldiers have never been my thing. Too uptight." One corner of her mouth quirked. "I prefer my guys less restrained. And with less clothing."

I suppressed a grin and the rumble building in my chest. "I'm glad you do not have a fetish for helmets."

A pair of nearly identical females with pink skin and a long platinum hair crossed the sand in front of us hand in hand with a Vandar warrior whose battle kilt hung off his hips at a precarious angle. His expression was dazed, and his dark hair tousled as the females led him to a nearby cabana and laid him onto the bed. I looked away as one of the alien females dipped her head under his kilt while the other straddled his face.

"You weren't kidding when you said this pleasure planet was different from the others. This is nothing like the dodgy one near Jengon 5." Alana readjusted her hand in mine as we walked down the steps onto the beach. "I'm glad you decided to bring me with you."

"It was unfair to treat my crew to a respite from the ship and not you." I spotted the Laurinian female standing at the edge of the sand near a staircase cut into the alabaster rock. Instead of being barely dressed, she wore a white robe that reached her feet and had an attached hood she pushed back at our approach. "At your suggestion, I have made arrangements for us to sample what the city has to offer."

She swung her head to me. "I thought you weren't into sharing."

My boots faltered in the sand. "Sharing?"

"You did say sample, right?"

I looked up at the cliffs. "The environments and villas. Not the pleasures." I squeezed her hand. "I thought we agreed that we would not be in need of the female pleasurers?"

"I guess another guy would be out of the question?"

I scowled at her before seeing her teasing expression.

She let out a low whistle. "Note to myself. Vandar don't even like to joke about sharing their women."

"No, we do not." Even the idea of sharing her with another male made a growl escape my throat.

Alana laughed. "You aren't going to throw me over your shoulder again, are you?"

"Do not provoke me," I said, but gave her a half smile.

The Laurinian female bowed as she joined us at the base of the stairs, her white robe swirling around her legs as she moved. "You must be Raas Bron. We are grateful for your patronage." She handed me a flat disc. "I think you will be pleased with the penthouse villa we've prepared for you and your…" Her eyes shifted to Alana briefly, "companion."

"Thank you." I inclined my head at her, taking the disc and memorizing the directions she gave me to the top of the cliffs.

Alana tipped her head back. "The penthouse?"

"It is not as difficult a walk as you might imagine." The Laurinian smiled at us, prodded us to step on the bottom step and then touched her hand to a shiny white post to one side.

Suddenly, the steps—which had appeared to be cut into the stone—began to move. I wrapped an arm around Alana for balance as we were propelled up, twisting back and forth across the rock face as we rose higher. When we'd reached the top, the moving steps deposited us before a clear door.

I glanced at the disc in my hand, then noticed that a circle in the transparent door glowed blue. Pressing the disc to the circle, I watched as it hummed and flashed a series of lights before the door swung open.

Alana stepped inside and sighed. "I get why your guys like pleasure planets so much."

The inside of the villa was as gleaming white as the cliffs, with shiny floors topped with fluffy rugs. A round, glass table held an array of glistening fruits—most of which were unfamiliar to me—and a bottle of something chilled in a clear bowl piled high with ice.

There was little furniture, but a large, flat, bed, with a skylight above it, took up the center of the room. The space opened up onto a balcony and then a pool that dangled out beyond the cliffs, the blue water sparkling as the rays from two distant suns bounced off the surface.

"Most pleasure planets are not like this," I said, marveling at the luxury, and wondering how this jewel had managed to elude our notice before.

Alana plucked a shiny, purple berry from a tray and popped it in her mouth. "The Raas quarters are pretty nice, but this is amazing."

The mingled moans of other couples in villas drifted up from below.

"Normally I wouldn't be into listening to your friends fuck, but in this setting it feels pretty normal," Alana continued, with a laugh.

I came up behind her, wrapping my arms around her and cupping her breasts in my hands. "I'm glad you don't mind."

She rolled her head back. "As long as you don't mind them hearing us."

Desire coiled in my belly as I thumbed her nipples between my fingers and ran my tail up the inside of her leg. "That is the only thing of you that I do not mind sharing."

CHAPTER THIRTY-SIX

Alana

Padding naked across the room, I paused at the table and dropped a sedative pill into Bron's half-drunk glass of wine. I watched it dissolve, then sat on the edge of the pool and dangled my legs into the water, moaning at the delicious warmth.

"It's heated," I called over my shoulder to Bron, who was stretched across the bed on his stomach.

He lifted his head lazily and then dropped it again, grunting at me.

I laughed and slipped all the way into the water. "Don't tell me I've worn you out already, Raas."

"Is this how you killed people?" He rolled over onto his back and stared at the skylight in the ceiling. "You fucked them to death?"

Even though he was teasing me, I flinched at his words. The reality was I'd killed many males after I'd fucked them. Some I'd killed while they were still inside me. I lowered myself so that the warm water enveloped my shoulders. "Is that how you wish to die, Raas?"

His chuckle was warm and deep. "For a Vandar, the most honorable death is in battle. But I might reconsider spending eternity in Zedna with Lokken if the alternative was to spend it with my cock buried inside you."

I stretched my arms wide under the water, pulling them hard and propelling myself to the clear side that hung out over the cliff. Peering beneath me, my legs scissored above the transparent pool bottom. Below that were alabaster rocks, extending to the pink curve of sand, and the sea-green bay.

My pulse fluttered at the sheer drop and the sensation that there was nothing beneath me, but I crossed my arms, resting them on the pool's ledge, and gazed out across the horizon. The two suns that warmed the planet were sinking into the sea, sending a warm glow across the water and making it appear as if it was on fire.

I sighed as I took in the idyllic scene. I'd spent most of my life moving from target to target, with stops at outposts and imperial colonies to refuel and resupply. But I'd never been somewhere like this, or allowed myself to be fully immersed in anything that wasn't an assignment.

I twisted my head to look at the alien warlord lying on the bed. I'd also never felt about anyone the way I felt about Bron. Even though truly being with him was impossible, I couldn't ignore the way he made me feel. I turned back around abruptly, despising myself for what I'd done.

"Come back to bed," he called.

"You come in the water," I teased, giving him an arch smile over my shoulder. "And bring our wine with you."

He lifted himself so he was propped on his elbows and eyed me.

"You do swim, don't you?" I asked, flipping over and hooking my arms over the pool's ledge.

"How many pools have you seen on our warbird?"

I thought about that and the depth of his bathing pools. There was no swimming required when all you had to do to save yourself from drowning was stand up. "Come on. It's not hard. I'll teach you."

He grumbled as he rolled to the side of the bed and stood.

Even though I'd seen him naked more times than I could count, it was hard to tear my eyes from him as he walked across the room, plucked the two glasses off the table, downed the rest of his wine before putting the glass back down, and continued to the pool's edge. There wasn't a micron on him that wasn't muscle, aside from the long cock that swung between his legs and made my throat tighten.

I choked back a laugh when he'd lowered himself into the pool and the water still only reached his chest. "I don't think you need to know how to swim in here. You can just walk."

The Raas grinned as he took long steps through the water toward me, holding out my glass of wine.

"Thanks." I took a sip and tried not to think of the sedative pill—the last one I'd had hidden on me when I was taken—and the drugs that were making their way through the Vandar's system. I swallowed and set the glass on the wide lip of the pool.

Bron braced his arms on the clear wall on either side of me, leaning forward and pinning me beneath him. "You're right.

Swimming isn't hard."

I rolled my eyes at him. "At least you're out of bed."

"Not everything requires a bed." He bent his head to mine and nipped at my neck, sending tingles of desire skating down my spine.

Although we were at the top of the cliff, the pool was completely in the open, which sent a forbidden thrill through me. I let my legs float up until they could circle his waist, then I hooked my hands around the back of his head. "Anyone can see us out here."

"Maybe I want them to see us," Bron whispered in my ear. "Maybe I want everyone to see me claiming you. Then there will be no doubt that you're mine."

The hard points of my nipples brushed his chest, as I arched into him. "I'm pretty sure everyone on your ship knows you've been fucking me."

"Mmmm." He kissed his way down my throat then wrapped an arm around my back, lifting my chest out of the water. He sucked each firm nipple hard before dragging the tip of his tail through my folds. "Not the same thing."

I tightened my grip around his neck. "Then show them."

He raised his head to meet my eyes, his lips quirking up as he pushed into me slow and deep, the thick fur sending tingles ricocheting through my body. "No fair using your tail."

He stroked it in and out. "Who said I had to play fair?"

I let my head fall back, the water sloshing over the side of the pool as the Raas thrust again and again. The forbidden excitement of being watched and the thrill of having the alien's tail fucking me made my release build quickly.

"Eyes on me, Alana," he said as my moans became more desperate and as he seamlessly slid his tail out of me and his cock in.

I met his gaze as the hard bar of his cock powered into me, the water churning around us. His pupils were huge and black, pinning me with their feverish intensity. My hands slipped to his shoulders, my nails scoring his flesh as my release crashed over me, the tremors rocking my body like punishing waves and rippling around his cock.

With a final raw sound, Bron surged inside me. A bellow was ripped from his lips as his shaft pulsed hot and urgent. Then he sagged against me.

"Raas?" I said when his weight started to pull me under.

He looked up at me, but his eyes were unfocused. The drugs were working.

"Come on," I said. "Let's get back in bed."

"Greedy," he murmured, as I led him up the stairs at the far end of the pool and across the room. "You've already had my tail and my cock."

"No," I said under my breath as I propelled him to the bed, and he collapsed onto it. "Sneaky."

"Alana," he said, fighting to keep his eyes open as he reached for me.

I took his hand, leaning in to kiss him one last time before sitting back and watching his eyes close. "I'm so sorry, Bron. One day you'll realize that I did this to save you."

I took a shaky breath, steeling myself for what I needed to do, and searching the floor for my clothes. Then the walls of the villa trembled.

CHAPTER THIRTY-SEVEN

Svar stood at his console on the command deck, scanning the readouts as he swayed back and forth, and let the flaps of his battle kilt knock against his thighs. He was still thinking about the eager Laurinian who'd wrapped her lips so prettily around his cock. If he closed his eyes, he could almost imagine himself back in the cabana bed, the salty air warm on his face and the female's tongue hot and wet. He'd tangled his fingers in her thick blue hair as she'd sucked him, watching his length disappear into her mouth and her cheeks hollow.

"*Tvek.*" He pushed down his aching cock with one hand, shaking his head and trying to banish the distracting thoughts of the pleasurer. At least he was the only warrior on the command deck, although he doubted any of his fellow raiders would fault him for lingering thoughts after a visit to a pleasure planet like Laurinia.

The planet itself had been almost as much of an indulgence as the female, the warmth of the sun and the soft sounds of the lapping water seducing him just as completely. Watching the pleasurer move up and down on him, her bare breasts bouncing as he'd watched boats hover across the water in the distance, had been an intoxicating sight he wouldn't soon forget.

A sharp beep drew his attention to his screen, and he forced the memory of the hedonistic planet from his mind. A transmission was coming in. He peered closer, not sure if he was reading it correctly. Were the Valox resistance ships they'd assisted really sending them a transmission? His stomach clenched. An encrypted transmission.

Tapping the console, he tensed as the voice of one of the Valox fighters filled the room, crackling with interference.

"Vandar horde." The voice broke, and it was clear that the speaker was having difficulty breathing. "This is Captain Brandon of the Valox resistance." He coughed. "I'm sending you this encrypted message on a secure channel in hopes it reaches you in time."

In time? Svar grasped the corners of his console, willing the speaker to talk faster.

"After we parted, our fleet was again attacked by imperial forces."

Another gurgling cough all but told Svar the man was choking on his own blood. He clenched his hands tighter, hate for the Zagrath rising up hot in his own chest.

"Most of our ships were destroyed, and our fighters killed." The captain paused. "But not before they were tortured."

Svar shifted from one foot to the other, needing to move but fighting the urge to hit something. The Zagrath were like a plague, making its victims writhe in pain before inflicting the ultimate punishment. A plague that he and his people were systematically fighting to destroy.

"I'm sending you this message because I fear they extracted certain information from one of our fighters." The transmission broke up, the words garbled before they resumed. "There is a chance the empire knows about the human female on your horde."

Svar's blood went cold. The female? The one Raas Bron had claimed as his? The one who was currently on the surface of Laurinia with him?

The *majak* shook his head, but he knew there could be no other female. There were no other females on their horde. The other human females on Vandar hordes were far away in other sectors. He didn't know how the Valox had learned of the female— perhaps a careless slip of the tongue by one of their raiders when they'd offered assistance. It didn't matter now. The empire knew.

He blew out a breath and forced himself to think calmly. The female Raas Bron had taken was not the first human to be claimed by a Vandar. He choked out a dark laugh. Actually, it was becoming more frequent than he ever would have expected.

There was no reason that this female should bring the attention of the empire, Svar reasoned. Even if she had been running from them.

"If this information brings danger to your horde, I am sincerely sorry," the captain continued. "You offered us aid when we needed it, and you have my eternal gratitude." He coughed out a mirthless laugh. "Though I doubt I have much longer to make good on that promise."

A wave of pity for the dying captain made Svar press his lips together. "Have no fear, captain." He vowed. "We will rain fire on the empire for what they've done to you."

"I am the only Valox ship that escaped, although I suspect they let me go because they know life support on board is failing." He sucked in a tight breath. "In their last warning to me, I could hear

Zagrath in the background saying that they would find the human and punish her for her betrayal."

Svar straightened. "Betrayal?"

"They mentioned Laurinia and they were discussing a trap." The captain's voice faded. "I hope you know what that means, and I hope this reaches you before they do."

Svar froze in place as the transmission devolved into more coughing and spluttering and finally an agonizing death gasp. When the line was static, he jerked his head up to the view screen and the idyllic planet of Laurinia. It was a trap?

He shook his head, not wanting to believe the warning. Was it possible their horde had flown right into the clutches of the empire without knowing it? No, surely not.

Svar studied his scans again. There was nothing.

Wait. His eye caught on a faint dot pulsing just on the edge of the screen. Within moments, it raced across the star chart, other dots joining it to surround the planet. The empire was fast approaching with what appeared to be an entire fleet.

Activating a ship-wide red alert, Svar called all raiders to their battle stations as the first laser fire volleyed from the Zagrath ships, his fingers buzzing with the fervor of impending bloodshed. Then he turned and ran for the hangar deck.

The battle they'd all been wishing for had finally come, and their horde was not ready.

CHAPTER THIRTY-EIGHT

Alana

The rumble was faint at first, then I was pitched to the side. I caught myself on the table as the trays of food clattered to the floor.

What the hell?

I looked out onto the horizon which had been so peaceful only moments before. The pink sky was now filled with red beams shooting down from above. Was the planet seriously under attack? It only took me a moment to realize that it was the empire, and they were coming for me. Who else would unleash such firepower on a pleasure planet?

"We have to go!" I shouted to Bron, then turned to see him unconscious on the bed.

Fuck me. I wasn't sure how long the drugs would take to wear off —the Vandar were bigger than anyone I'd used the sedatives on before—but at the moment, he was gone. And I couldn't leave him. Not with the imperial forces firing and us being on the top of a cliff. One direct hit and the entire mountain would crumble.

Panic and anger were like rocket fuel storming through my veins. I hurriedly pulled on my clothes, stumbling as the blasts continued to rattle the villa. Then I jumped on the bed and shook Bron by the shoulders.

"Wake up, babe," I begged, slapping his cheeks so sharply they turned pink.

He blinked groggily, frowning up at me. "That hurts."

I was so happy he was conscious, I kissed him hard on the lips. "I know. I'm sorry. Listen, you can spank me for it later." I spotted his kilt on the floor and scooped it up. "Right now, we need to get the fuck out of here before we're blown to bits."

"We just got here." His words were slurred as he shook his head, then he stopped and grinned. "Did you say I can spank you?"

"That's what you took from what I said?" I huffed out an impatient breath as I tugged his kilt on over his feet and up the length of his muscular legs. "If we get out of here alive, you can do anything you want to me."

His smile widened, but I snapped a finger to focus his attention. "But right now, you need to get dressed and follow me. Okay?"

The villa shook, this time harder, and dust sifted down from above. Bron's brow creased. "Is that laser fire?"

"Yep." I pulled him up by the arms, astounded by just how heavy he was. "Imperial laser fire, if I'm right."

He stiffened, his eyes snapping into focus. "The Zagrath? Here?"

"Unless your horde has decided to fire on the planet." I jerked his kilt up around his waist and sat back, heaving.

Bron stood, his gaze sweeping the sky as red beams slashed across it. It was as if the mention of his enemy had wiped all the fog from his brain, although I suspected adrenaline and the sheer size of him helped. He hooked his battle axe on his waist and held out his hand to me. "Come on."

I took it without argument, and we moved toward the door, although I noticed his step wasn't as fast or sure as usual. I latched my arm around his waist as he leaned against the door frame to draw a breath. He glanced down at me. "When we're back safely on my ship, I look forward to you explaining why I feel like I've been hit in the head by a Rurali ice monster."

I swallowed hard, grateful for the distraction of the shaking planet. "I didn't—"

He snapped up a hand. "Not now. Now we need to get out. Later you will explain yourself—and it had better be good."

Pressing my lips together, I stuck my head out of the doorway. Luckily, the blasts had disabled the locks and shaken the door off its hinges. I saw no imperial soldiers, so I led Bron out of the villa and onto the top of the stairs. Instead of spiraling us down to the beach, they remained like stone.

"The blast must have knocked out some of their systems." I cursed under my breath at the thought of trying to walk down hundreds of steps with an unsteady Vandar raider.

Bron put out a hand as I started to take a step down. "It's too late."

I followed his gaze to the swath of pick sand where small imperial transport ships were touching down. My stomach lurched as the all too familiar helmeted fighters ran off them and fanned out across the beach and toward the cliffs.

"We go up," he said, motioning above us. "*Vaes.*"

Up? I swallowed hard, although I knew we had no choice. Not with the Zagrath forces running up the steps with alarming speed.

I nodded, wishing I had a weapon on me. The Raas had his battle axe, but if the enemy caught us, I had nothing but my fighting skills. Not that my hand to hand skills weren't impressive, especially against the imperial soldiers, who were better with blasters, but my fingers itched for a blade.

Raas Bron's pace quickened as we rushed up the steps, his energy obviously fueled by fury. Instead of bare rock at the top of the cliffs, I was surprised to see a series of flat-topped buildings with neat paths winding through them. As we rushed past the structures, I peeked through the windows and saw homey rooms with colorful linens and vanity tables strewn with brushes and pots of pigment. Then it hit me. This was where the pleasurers lived.

I tugged hard on Bron's hand to stop him, and he glanced back at me, his gaze questioning.

"If they catch me, they'll execute me," I said, nodding to one of the small houses. "I need a disguise."

He cut his eyes to his own battle kilt hanging low on his hips, his skin still damp from the pool. "I doubt there is any disguise that will hide me."

I looked him up and down then pulled him behind me into one of the small houses. "Never say never."

CHAPTER THIRTY-NINE

Bron

My head throbbed as I gaze up at the female draped in layers of diaphanous fabric. The jeweled edge of the face veil sparkled as she leaned closer, her brown eyes the only part of her face visible behind layers of pink and lavender.

"Raas," she whispered.

I attempted to roll away from her. Where was I, and why was a pleasurer on top of me?

Sitting up, a hood fell away from my head. I glanced down at myself. And why was I dressed in the white robes of the Laurinians?

"Bron," the female said, putting a hand on my arm as I tried to stand. "It's me. Don't you remember where we are?"

I swung my gaze to her, as she unhooked one side of her veil to reveal the bottom half of her face. *Alana.*

I did remember where we were. I'd brought her to the surface of the pleasure planet, and we'd been in our suite. Then I'd fallen asleep and…

"The Zagrath." My heart clenched. "They're here."

"Not yet," Alana said, standing and crossing to the window, her multicolor, sheer skirt swishing. "We came in here to disguise ourselves, and you passed out again."

I touched a hand to my temple. Passed out? That's right. I hadn't fallen asleep.

"You did this." I fought down a wave of nausea. "It's your fault I feel so weak. Did you do all this to set a trap for me?"

"No!" She swiveled around to face me. "Yes. I'm the reason you're so zonked out, but I had nothing to do with the imperial invasion."

My head was heavy and the words sluggish on my lips. "Why should I believe you?"

She put her hands on her hips, the diaphanous sleeves of her dress fluttering. "Because they're here to kill me, too. If I'd called the Zagrath, why would I be running from them? If I was behind this, all I'd have to do would be wave my arms and let them take you down."

I stood quickly, grabbing her by the wrist and pinning her to the wall next to the window. "You expect me to believe you after what you've just done?"

"I'm so sorry. You have to believe that I didn't want to hurt you." Her chest heaved as she peered up at me.

I shook my head to rid myself of the lingering sluggishness. "Drugging me wasn't hurting me?"

"I thought I was saving you. The only thing I've ever been doing since I realized I couldn't kill you is trying to keep *you* from getting killed. I knew the empire would come after me with everything they had. I told you before, Bron. I'm a liability to you."

I searched her face and saw no deception. "Maybe, but you're also mine to protect."

"But I'm not." Tears glittered in her eyes. "I know you want to protect me, but I'm not yours. I don't have your marks, and I probably never will. I've done too many horrible things to ever be anyone's true mate."

I shook my head, but she put a hand over my mouth.

"It's okay. I love you for wanting to protect me. No one's ever done that for me." She tightened her jaw. "But now it's time for me to protect you and leave your horde. You'll be safer without me and without the empire hunting for me."

I pushed her hand off my mouth, clasping her wrist and bringing it to my lips, kissing the soft skin and feeling the trill of her pulse. "I can't do that, Alana. It is done."

"What's done?"

"This." I looked intently at her. "You and me. There's no undoing what I feel for you or what you feel for me. It's too late."

Her gaze darted to the door as sounds of battle drifted up from the cliffs below. "It's not too late. Let me go and draw their fire. They'll follow me, and leave your raiders alone."

Dropping her wrist, I lowered my lips to hers, kissing her softly. "Do you really think I could ever let you go?"

She whimpered as her lips sank into mine, kissing me back with a sad yearning. When she pulled away, she blinked up at me. "You'd rather die than let me go?"

I cupped her face in one hand, stroking the pad of my thumb across her jawline. "I would rather have a valiant death defending the female I love, than live a life of emptiness without her." I shrugged. "Besides, eternal life in Zedna with the old gods is not such a bad fate."

The noise of battle grew louder.

"Any chance I can hitch a ride with you to Zedna?" Alana asked, giving me a weak smile.

My heart squeezed as I memorized the lines of her face and the curve of her lips. Then my eyes wandered to the dark lines curling up her throat beneath the sheer fabric of the veil.

"Alana." The word was choked as I gaped at her, then tore at her veil.

She let out a small yelp, looking down at the bare skin I'd exposed—skin that was emblazoned with my mating marks. We were both silent for a moment, then I opened the white robe covering my chest.

Alana sucked in a breath. "Your marks are…growing."

A swell of possessive pride filled my chest. "We will share the same marks. There will be no doubt to anyone who sees that you truly belong to me."

Her stunned expression didn't change, so I grabbed her by the shoulders.

She finally tipped her head back and locked her eyes on mine. "It's been so long since I mattered to anyone."

"You more than matter to me," I said, pressing a palm to her marks, the heat of her flesh making my own skin ignite. "You are my mate. You are my world. And I won't let anyone take you from me for even a second."

She hitched in a breath and drew herself up to her full height. "Then we have some Zagrath ass to kick."

I grinned at her. "That's my bad little assassin."

"When I'm killing Zagrath, you can call me Mantis."

CHAPTER FORTY

Alana

Bron tossed off the white cloak as we ran from the house, but there was no time for me to change from the elaborate silks of the pleasurer. But it was better if my appearance confused them, so I hooked my veil across my face.

"Stay behind me," Raas Bron growled, as the thudding footsteps on stone grew louder.

I laughed, stepping out from behind him. "As if."

He opened his mouth to argue, then groaned and shook his head. "What did I do to earn such a stubborn mate?"

"I'm assuming that's rhetorical, or would you like a list of reasons?"

He gave me another tortured look and pulled me with him into a tight alley between the houses.

"The element of surprise," I said, nudging him in the ribs. "Good thinking."

There was no time for him to respond as the first imperial soldier crested the top of the cliff. Sun glinted off the familiar helmets as the faceless fighters ran up two-by-two, their crisp, smoke-blue uniforms out of place in the idyllic setting.

"I would say to wait until we see the whites of their eyes," Bron whispered, "but in this case, that won't work."

"Watch this," I said, stepping in front of them before he could stop me.

The soldiers skidded to a stop, clearly startled by the appearance of a Laurinian pleasurer.

"The Vandar warlord ran up there." I waved a hand toward a narrow passageway a few houses down.

The lead soldier nodded, and they ran forward, not even glancing to the side where Bron stood.

"One good thing about the imperial helmets," I told him as I waited until the soldiers had passed us. "They can't hear for shit."

When the last soldier had entered the narrow alley, Bron ran forward, slashing at their backs with his axe. Since they were pinned in, he was able to mow them down before the ones at the front even noticed or heard.

"Stupid helmets," I muttered, then spun around as I heard more fighters coming over the top.

They hesitated when they saw me, then stopped fully when Bron emerged from the alley with blood dripping from his blade. He walked to stand next to me, and I gave them a wide smile.

With a yell, the Zagrath soldiers surged forward. My heart pounded, and my hands tingled with excitement. This is what I'd been missing—a real fight.

The Raas swung his axe wide, knocking down the first soldiers. I dodged blaster fire, dipping low and sweeping my leg out and sending two fighters to the ground. When one dropped his blaster and it skittered across the stone, I dove for it.

I closed my fingers around the familiar, cool metal, spinning and firing at the imperial forces battling Bron. My aim hadn't suffered from lack of practice, my chest shots killing several instantly.

Bron glanced at me and grinned. "Nice shooting."

"We can't all be badasses with a battle axe."

We couldn't celebrate for long. More soldiers appeared from the stairs, rushing forward. Bron deflected their blaster fire while I fired off as many shots as I could.

Suddenly pain seared across my shoulder, and I dropped the blaster. Glancing at my bloody sleeve, I quickly assessed that it wasn't a deep wound, but it was bleeding, and I couldn't see where the blaster had fallen.

Ducking low, I ran for one of the alleys as heat scorched across the top of my head.

"Son of a bitch," I said. Another millimeter, and I'd have been dead.

I held a hand over my wound as I sucked in a breath. I needed to get back out there and help Bron. Tearing off my face veil, I tied it above my shoulder wound, using my teeth to pull the knot tight and staunch the blood.

"That should hold it." Now I needed to locate a blaster and help Bron. No way was he going to have all the fun.

An imperial soldier stepped into the alleyway, blocking my path. "I thought that was you." Instead of shooting me, he pulled off his helmet and tossed it to the ground.

I squinted at the Zagrath with dirty blond hair cut short and icy blue eyes. It was the one who'd given me the bruises before I'd left to be captured by the Vandar. The one who'd enjoyed hurting me way too much.

"You," I said, spitting out the word.

He gave me a leering smile. "Remember me, do you, sweetheart?"

"I'm not your sweetheart." I fisted my hands by my side. "But, yeah, I remember you. You were on my list of people to kill. Thanks for coming here and making it easier."

He laughed. "You think you're going to kill me? You're the most wanted person in the galaxy. There's a bounty on your head so large you'll never make it off this planet, much less out of this alley."

I gave him a hard smile. "We'll see."

His gaze moved down my body. "I have to say, Mantis. I like your new clothes. Is that what Vandar whores wear?"

Rage coursed through me, but I didn't respond. I was too busy trying to figure out how I was going to kill a Zagrath fighter who was armed with a blaster, when I had nothing but a grudge and a wounded arm.

"Don't want to tell me?" He shook his head as he advanced on me. "I don't blame you. If I'd been whoring myself to the enemy, I wouldn't want to admit it, either."

I wanted to yell for Bron, but I could hear him grunting as he fought off the other soldiers, their blaster fire ricocheting through the air. If I called out for help, it might distract him in his battle, which could mean death.

The fighter lunged for me. I jumped up and spun in midair, kicking out and landing a blow to his chest. He staggered back, but remained upright, cursing at me.

"You want to hit me again?" I yelled. "Come and get it."

"I don't want to hit you this time." He spit onto the ground. "I'm going to fuck you raw."

I narrowed my eyes at him. "Over my dead body."

He cracked his neck as he moved toward me. "That works for me."

I backed away, but kept my low battle stance. I needed to get away from this guy and find a blaster. If I could run fast enough and circle around to the battle, I should be able to get a blaster off one of the dead soldiers. That is, if this asshole didn't shoot me in the back.

I drew in a breath. It didn't matter. I had to try. Spinning on my heel, I took off running, keeping my head low in case he fired. But instead of blaster fire, all I heard was the pounding of his feet behind mine. Then a strong arm hooked around my waist, and I was flying backward.

He threw me to the ground, landing on top of me and pinning my arms to my side. I gasped for breath, but the wind had been knocked out of me. I could only open and close my mouth, as he pressed his body on top of mine. His breath was hot and desperate, as he fumbled with my skirts while roughly nudging my legs apart.

I managed to regain my breath enough to struggle against him, but he was too heavy, and I was still weak. I gathered all the breath I could and screamed, "Bron!"

The soldier's movements halted for a second, then he crushed his mouth to mine. Even though I knew it was to keep me from screaming again, his lips were punishing as they groped me. I opened my mouth, finding his tongue and biting down.

He reared back and backhanded me across the cheek. "Bitch!"

Even though the slap brought tears to my eyes, I used his momentary distraction to bring my knee up hard between his legs. While he gasped in pain, I scrambled to my knees. I didn't get far before he'd pulled me back, this time forcing me onto my stomach with my face shoved into the gritty stone. He shoved my skirts up as he fumbled to part my legs again. Fear clawed in my throat as I jerked up and tried to head butt him.

He dodged me and slammed my head back down. "Nice try, but it's time you pay for betraying the empire." He emitted a cruel laugh. "And I'm not going to be gentle."

Something hard pressed between my legs, and then his full weight was on me, forcing my breath out again. I braced myself for more as I attempted to draw a breath, but instead, something sticky trickled down my neck. Then the weight of his body was gone, and there was panting behind me.

I craned my neck, hoping it was not another imperial soldier.

CHAPTER FORTY-ONE

Bron

The imperial fighters came at me fast and hard, pouring over the top of the cliff like scurrying Jerpithian ants. They had blasters drawn, but I was faster with my battle axe, blocking their fire and causing the beams to ricochet away from me. When they came closer, I crouched low and swiped out, taking out an entire row of them below the knees. The soldiers coming up after them stumbled over the writhing bodies of Zagrath clutching their bloody stumps. I used the distraction to take off a few of their heads, the shiny helmets flying through the air and landing on the rock with a crack.

Between the screams of agony and the rushing of my own blood in my ears, I could hear little but the battle. Until her voice pierced through the grunting and wailing. Alana was calling my name.

Spinning around, I scoured the top of the cliff for her. She'd been right by my side when the fight had begun. Now, she was nowhere to be seen.

I ducked as blaster fire rained over me, slicing my axe through the air to take out the last soldiers rushing toward me. Then I held my breath, my chest burning, and listened again. There it was. The sound of furious grunts and Zagrath curses.

I ran toward the noise, slipping down an alleyway and spotting the imperial solider first. He was straddling Alana, his hand forcing her head down while he fumbled with his pants and kneed her legs open. Her skirts were pushed up around her waist and her ass was bare.

Fury drove me forward, my vision clouded with red rage as I swung my axe high and brought it down between the soldier's shoulder blades. A sharp breath was expelled from his chest, along with a bubble of blood from his mouth as he twisted around to look up at me with shocked eyes before slumping forward.

Lifting the body off Alana, I jerked my bloody blade from his back, then tossed his corpse aside like the trash it was.

She swiveled her head to me, her eyes still wild with panic and anger. When she saw me and then the dead Zagrath, she squeezed her eyes shut.

I calmed my own ragged breath as I knelt beside her. Although I wanted to kill a thousand Zagrath to pay for what they'd done to her, I'd have to settle for the dead body bleeding out beside me. And I'd have to quell my rage in order to comfort her.

I pulled her skirts down and noted that her knees were bloody. If I could have killed the man a second time, I would have. Instead I brushed a tangle of hair out of her eyes. "Did he hurt you badly?"

Alana shook her head even though her hands were trembling. "You came."

Curling an arm around her waist, I pulled her up. "I will always come for you."

She leaned into me for a moment, her body warm against mine. Then she cut her gaze to the unmoving imperial soldier. "I'm glad you killed him."

"The pleasure was all mine."

Alana laughed weakly. "I believe you."

Taking her face in my hands, I wiped away a trickle of blood from her bottom lip. "The empire has no claim on you anymore." I lowered my mouth to hers, feathering my lips across her bruised one. "You are mine."

When she pulled back to meet my eyes, she shook her head, resting her fingers on the hot marks etching my collarbone. "We are each other's."

I nodded, my throat tightening as I kissed her again.

Before I could fully lose myself in the feel and taste of her, a loud whoosh overhead made us both look up. A ship was descending through the atmosphere and hovering over the cliffs. Correction —a fleet of ships. This was either very good or very bad.

I handed Alana a blaster I'd tucked into my belt. "Ready to get out of here?"

She gave me a sharp nod. "And take out some imperial soldiers along the way, right?"

My mate amazed me. Even though she was bruised and bloodied, she still welcomed the fight. "You will make an excellent Vandar."

We ran down the alley, and I held out a hand to hold her back so I could assess the situation. I'd managed to take out all the fighters who'd come up from below, but if the ships from above were depositing more soldiers, I didn't want us running into an ambush. I saw nothing, so I rushed out with my battle axe clutched in one hand, and her hand held tight in the other.

The street was littered with dead bodies, the scent of blood and burned flesh making my nose twitch. I ignored them and the fact that I'd killed them all.

I needed to get Alana off the planet and to safety, but there would undoubtably be more fighters coming up from below. A rush of hot air from behind made me turn and hold my weapon high. But when I saw the shiny black of the hull, I almost cried out in relief.

The raider ship touched down and the ramp lowered, my *majak* rushing off with a squad of screaming Vandar behind him.

"Svar!" Relief coursed through my body at the sight of my first officer and more raiders itching for battle.

He spotted me and ran forward, while the rest of the raiders fanned out to meet the Zagrath soldiers as they crested the cliffs. "Raas. You are alive!"

I gestured to the bodies strewn behind me. "Not because the empire did not try hard enough."

Svar made a face. "Imperial automatons against a Raas of the Vandar? Was there ever much doubt who would prevail?"

I clapped a hand on his shoulder. "Tell me what is happening, *majak*. How did they find us?"

Svar let out a breath, his face contorting into a grimace. "The Valox resistance was attacked again. When the Zagrath tortured them, one of their fighters revealed the presence of a human female on our horde. The empire figured it out from there."

I pulled Alana closer. "So this was not an attack on us as much as an attempt to eliminate my mate?"

Svar glanced at Alana then his gaze dropped to the ground. "It seems so, Raas. As soon as I found out, I alerted the entire horde and sent reinforcements to the surface. We have beaten back their fleet, Raas, and destroyed the lead battleship. They are in full retreat."

I scanned the helmeted soldiers still emerging from the stairs. "So these remaining imperial fighters?"

"Have been abandoned." Svar's lip curled in obvious derision. Vandar never left raiders behind.

I squared my shoulders. "Once we have killed them all and returned all our raiders to our horde ships, we are going after the rest of the fleeing imperial fleet. The empire needs to learn that if they threaten a Raas' mate, they will pay with their lives."

"It is done." My *majak* clicked his heel sharply.

I hooked my axe onto my belt and swung Alana up into my arms, ignoring her protests. "*Vaes.* Let's go home."

CHAPTER FORTY-TWO

Alana

"Do I really need to be blindfolded?" I touched my fingers to the thick cloth covering my eyes.

"I know you, mate," Bron's velvet voice rumbled in my ear. "You are too curious not to peek."

I huffed out a breath and leaned into him as the transport ship shuddered beneath my feet. Ever since we'd hunted down the imperial fleet that had attacked Laurinia and blown it out of the sky, our new course had been a thing of whispers. I didn't know where Raas Bron was taking me, but wherever it was, he was excited about it.

"Is it another pleasure planet?" I asked, drumming my fingers against his chest. "We were cruelly interrupted during our visit to the last one."

He barked out a laugh. "Before or after you drugged me and attempted to leave?"

My mouth fell open. "I explained that to you and apologized—a lot." My chest squeezed. Even now, thinking about what I'd done and what I'd been thinking made my face burn with shame. I couldn't imagine life without the Raas, and I was pretty sure it wouldn't have been a long one if I'd managed to escape from him.

He stroked a hand down my back. "And I accepted your apologies. I especially enjoyed the ones that involved you spread out beneath me with your legs—"

"Bron!" I swatted at him. It might just be the two of us as passengers on the transport, but there was at least a pilot, and I didn't need him to hear all about how enthusiastically I'd made up with the Raas.

"Why are you embarrassed? You are the mate of a Raas. If we did not spend every free moment in bed, my raiders would be concerned."

I shook my head. "I doubt they want to hear about it. Their time on the pleasure planet was cut short, as well."

"You make a good point. Perhaps I should order a stop at a pleasure planet once we have left here. Although they welcomed the battle, my raiders deserve some female entertainment that is not marred by the empire."

I tilted my head at him, even though I couldn't see him. "You don't mind if we sit this pleasure planet visit out, do you?"

He nuzzled against my neck. "Of course not. I have everything I need with you. You do still have that pleasurer's dress, don't you?"

I cringed. "The one ripped and covered in blood? I asked for that to be burned."

"Too bad. You looked very appealing in that face veil."

"I can't say the same about you in the white robe." I ran my hand down the hard bumps of his stomach and teased the skin beneath his belt. "I much prefer you in…less."

"Mmmmm." His contented hum was interrupted by the shift in the engines, and then the jolt of the transport touching down.

I grasped him to steady myself, my pulse fluttering in both excitement and nervousness. "I can't believe you're making me walk off this ship with a blindfold. This had better be some *tvekking* amazing surprise."

He emitted a low growl. "You keep using Vandar curse words like that, and I might have to take you against the wall before I can let you off this ship."

I put a hand to the cloth over my eyes. "Then I'm definitely ripping off the blindfold."

Raas Bron took both my hands in his as the ship's ramp touched down, the metal rattling. "No more waiting, mate."

He led me forward and then down the ramp. Even though he held my hands, my steps were tentative. Once we were off the ship, sunlight hit my face, along with a breeze that carried the scent of loamy soil. So we weren't on another ship. It was a planet. But which one, and why was it such a big deal?

"I did mention that I hate surprises, right?"

He dropped my hands and then fumbled with my blindfold. "Only about a thousand times."

When the fabric finally fell away, I blinked as my eyes adjusted to the light. Yep, it was definitely a planet. I spotted trees and a white sun burning high in the sky and… My breath caught in my throat.

"I know those mountains," I whispered, my gaze locked on a craggy range topped with snow in the distance. "This is Faaral."

"Yes," Bron said. "It's your home planet."

I opened my mouth to speak but memories washed over me, making it impossible.

"Does it look like you remember it?" Bron asked quietly.

I cleared my throat. "It does." I inhaled deeply. "It even smells the same."

I wrenched my gaze from the horizon and peered up at Bron. "I can't believe you did this."

"If I had a home planet I could visit, I would want to," he said. "Your world is still much as it would have been when you were taken." His expression darkened. "The empire seems to have left it alone, aside from occasional visits to take children."

As much as seeing Faaral provoked painful memories of being torn from my parents, it also made me feel happy. "I was happy here. Before. But I've never wanted to return. I was too scared of what I'd discover and afraid that I was too different to be recognized."

"The empire might have taken much of your life from you," Bron said. "But they don't get to write the rest of it for you."

I squeezed his hand, the warmth in my heart blooming. "No one has ever done anything for me like this. No one has ever loved me liked this."

Bron cupped my face in both his hands. "Vandar do not do anything halfway."

I choked out a teary laugh. "That's true enough."

"I love you with all of my heart, Alana." Bron tipped my face up and kissed me. "I pledge all of myself and all of my horde to you. Forever."

"I love you, Bron." As strange as it should have felt to tell anyone I loved them after I'd spent most of my life making sure not to get close to anyone, the words spilled naturally from my lips. "I can only offer you me, but you've got all of me."

This time when he kissed me, his mouth was searching, and I sank into the warmth and solidness of him. When he finally tore his lips from mine, he smiled down at me. "Ready for one more surprise?"

I nodded, breathless, taking his hand as he led me away from the transport and toward city gates that looked vaguely familiar, if not significantly more weathered.

"This was where I lived," I said, my voice cracking, and my heart thundering in my chest. "Just beyond these gates."

When I saw the two people standing just to the side of the stone gates, my knees wobbled. Raas Bron slid his arm around my waist to keep me upright as we continued forward, but my vision was too blurred to see anything but a flurry of arms, as my parents ran to me, wrapping me in their hugs as they sobbed. Tears streamed down my face as they held me, and a lifetime of loneliness fell away like discarded armor.

Even though Bron had stepped away, I still felt his love for me as he watched the reunion he'd so carefully planned. He'd given me something that, as an orphan, he could never have himself. He'd given me back my parents. As much as it must have brought him joy, I suspected there was also longing for what he could never bestow upon himself.

I pulled back from my parents to look at them and wipe away my tears through the smiles and laughter. Then I found Bron and locked my gaze on his.

"I'm guessing you already know Raas Bron?" I asked my parents, holding my hand out to him. "He's my—"

"Fiancé," he finished for me, giving a deep bow to both my parents. "With your blessing."

I cocked my eyebrow at him. He'd clearly read up on my people and their ancient traditions. The Vandar raider continued to be everything I needed, and none of the things he was rumored to be. He was, and would always be, my one true mate and my only true love. It seemed foolish now that I'd ever thought otherwise.

"Actually," I said, after my parents had thanked him and hugged him and thanked him again. "I'll be his Raisa, which means the mate of the Raas. So he's family now."

Raas Bron took my hand in his, turning it over and lifting my wrist to his lips, where he kissed it so delicately a shiver ran down my spine. "My Raisa."

Then I pulled him into a hug with both of my parents as they threw their arms around the big, tough Raas and showered him with kisses. Laughing at his flushed cheeks and embarrassed pleasure, I swiped away more tears. After being so alone for so long, I finally had a family again. And so did he.

EPILOGUE

Corvak

I stalked from one end of the room to the other, ignoring the view out the triangular window. There was nothing to see anyway. Nothing I hadn't seen when I'd been escorted to my new home.

"Not for long it isn't," I growled as I spun on my heel and stomped back toward the door.

I might have been exiled from my horde, but that didn't mean I was doomed to live the rest of my life on Kimithion III. I tore a hand through my hair, my body vibrating with rage as I thought about the planet I'd been dumped on.

Some might find the stark landscape of the planet, with its sharp mountain spires that jutted into the air and encircled expansive, turquoise shallows, to be appealing, but for me it was nothing more than a temporary prison.

I finally peered out of my quarters. The suns were sinking below the distant peaks, turning the sky a startling shade of purple. Stars had already begun to appear like faint dots as the last rays of pink light faded. For a Vandar raider who's spent most of life in the blackness of space, the colors and the light were another reminder that I was no longer on my horde ship or with my people.

The quarters I'd been given were built into the mountains, like all residences on the planet, and paths wound through the rock connecting the hollowed-out spaces like a maze. At least that felt familiar, as the inside of a Vandar warbird was a twisting labyrinth much like this rock-hewn city. But that was the only thing that reminded me of my horde. My horde that had left me and flown away.

Jerking my head from the setting suns, I sank onto the window ledge. As much as I wanted to hate Bron for what he'd done, I'd given the Raas no choice. I'd defied him and taken the female he'd claimed as his mate. Even thinking about it made my face flush with shame.

I'd been so convinced she was working for the empire. I'd been sure of her duplicity and certain that she was a threat to the horde. Sure enough to risk everything that mattered to me to prove it.

But I'd been wrong. At least, I hadn't found any reason to convince the Raas I was right, and she should not be trusted. I'd gambled when I'd challenged him—and I'd lost.

The battle with my former brother-in-arms flashed through my mind. I'd been a fool to challenge a sitting Raas, even one who'd recently been my equal. The horde did not tolerate insurrection or disloyalty. It couldn't.

The bitter taste of bile rose in my throat as I thought of being labeled a traitor by my people. Raas Kratos would not be surprised. He'd slapped down my challenges many times, but I suspected it was because we were cousins that he had never truly punished me. I had calculated wrong when I'd thought Bron would be as forgiving.

Even though I knew the Raas had been within his rights, rage still burned within me that he'd dumped me *here*—a pre-warp planet populated by humans and a native species that reminded me of overgrown Granthilian geckos, just on two feet instead of four. There was precious little technology, and virtually no weapons. The only reason the planet hadn't been taken by the Zagrath was the fact that it had little of value. The climate was arid and not useful for scalable farming, and the core contained no valuable minerals worth mining.

"I'd rather have been put out an airlock," I muttered under my breath.

My fuming was interrupted by a sharp rap at the door. The last thing I wanted was visitors, but since I was officially a guest on their world, I didn't have much choice.

I opened the door and was greeted by two males—one human and the other a native Kimitherian.

"Welcome Corvak of Vandar," the human said, giving me a tight smile.

The native who was covered in iridescent, greenish-blue scales blinked at me, the vertical pupil in his yellow eyes contracting. "We are happy to count you among us."

I doubted that was true. They'd been paid handsomely to take me, and although they weren't my jailors, we all knew it might be some time before I left their world.

"Thank you," I said, giving them both a small bow. It was clear these males were representatives of their community, if not the leaders. "I'm not sure what you've been told, but I assure you that I have no intention of being a disruption. You won't even know I'm here."

The human chuckled, rubbing his hands together. "I'm afraid that would be quite impossible. You're the only Vandar on the planet and the only trained warrior."

He had a point. I was at least a head taller than both of them, and while they were covered from head to toe in flowing robes, I still wore nothing but my battle kilt.

"I have no intention of fighting any of you," I said. "Despite what rumors you might have heard, my people do not battle against the innocent. Our only fight is against the empire and those who enable them."

"We know," the native said. "That is why we agreed to take you. We fear the empire will not ignore us forever."

I did not want to be blunt and point out that the empire could very well ignore them forever since their planet had nothing of value. I did have to coexist with these aliens, after all. "You fear an imperial attack?"

The human nodded, glancing over his shoulder. "Our hope is that you can train our males so we can defend ourselves."

"Did my Raas know of this?" I asked. If I didn't already want to kill Bron, I would have now.

"He assured us you would be the perfect Vandar to train our peoples in defense." The human inclined his head, as if acknowledging an uncomfortable truth. "Although he looked at me much as you do now when I expressed my fear."

"We have battled the Zagrath for many millennia," I said. "We understand how they operate. They will only attack if they can profit off your destruction."

The two aliens exchanged a wary look.

I huffed out a breath. "Is there something you did not tell Raas Bron?"

The native Kimitherian steepled his webbed hands and lifted them to his mouth. "There is something we have told no one, because it is too valuable and dangerous to be shared."

I folded my arms across my chest, highly doubting that this rocky planet contained anything requiring *this* much secrecy.

"It is the planet itself that's valuable," the human said. "Even we did not realize it at first, but it is why our two peoples have limited contact with others, and have kept our world from developing any technology that might draw interest."

"Your core contains nothing of value," I said. "Otherwise the empire would have established mines."

The two males exchanged another cautious look.

"*Tvek*," I growled, stroking a finger down my scar. "Tell me. Do not tell me. At this point, I'm starting not to care."

The Kimitherian bobbed his scaled head up and down. "You are right. If we want your help, we should be honest with you. Your leader did say you were honorable to a fault."

I flinched at the description. That sounded like something Bron would say.

"Kerl is nearly a thousand rotations old," the human said in a rush of words, glancing at the other male I assumed was named Kerl.

"Okay." I eyed them. "And one of your rotations is how many of our standard rotations?"

"That is in standard rotations," Kerl said, his yellow eyes fixed on me.

I took in that information. Humans had a life expectancy of eighty to a hundred standard rotations and Vandar closer to one hundred. "Your species is long-lived."

"It is not just my species," Kerl said. "Once the human settlers arrived, they too became immortal."

"Immortal?" I almost choked on the word.

The human smiled. "It isn't that we can't be killed. We can. We just don't seem to age on this planet."

I stared at them. "So the children I saw playing when I arrived?"

Kerl let out a laugh that was comprised of mostly clicks. "They are children. The aging seems to slow or stop once we reach our maturity."

I slid my gaze to the human. "How old are you…?"

"Terel," the man replied. "My name is Terel, and I'm three hundred and eleven years old."

I cocked my head at him. He looked no older than me.

"Do you understand now why we need to protect ourselves?" Kerl asked.

I did. "If anyone were to find out, they would…" I let my words die in my mouth.

"Remove us or kill us all," Terel said for me.

I gave a curt nod. It went without saying that the Zagrath would use such a planet to ensure their domination of the galaxy and ensure they never died. The thought of the imperial leadership living forever made my stomach churn.

"Who knows?" I asked, my defensive training kicking in.

"We hope no one." Kerl looked at Terel. "But we are not so foolish to think that can continue forever. Not with the empire taking over more planets for their outposts and colonies. We need to be able to defend ourselves."

I squared my shoulders, a new sense of purpose flaring inside me. "Then we have much work to do to train your people and prepare your defenses."

Sienna

"Where have you been?"

I paused on the window ledge as I swung a leg over and dipped my head inside, cursing to myself that I'd been busted again. I glanced up and saw my younger sister standing in the doorway to our bedroom. Her pale hair was backlit by the faint hallway light, giving her head a halo effect.

I rolled my eyes. If that wasn't fitting I didn't know what was. Juliette was the good one, always trying to keep me in line and usually failing at it.

"Nowhere important," I said, coming all the way inside and landing on the floor. "Just checking out the new resident."

"Sienna." She sighed. "You know father said we should steer clear of him. He's a Vandar."

The tips of my fingers tingled at the word. "I know. That doesn't mean he's going to bite."

She mumbled something about the raiders being vicious enough to drink their enemy's blood, but I only laughed.

"You've been listening to tall tales again. One Vandar can't possibly kill us all and drink our blood. And why would he? He's supposed to help us."

"Help us?" My sister's eyes widened, then narrowed at me. "Have you been sneaking around and eavesdropping again?"

"Only because no one ever tells us anything. Besides, I'm sure it won't be a secret for long that the Vandar is going to help train us to defend ourselves."

"Defend ourselves? From what? He's the only dangerous thing to come near our planet in a generation."

I flopped onto my bed. She was right about that. The Vandar they called Corvak was the most dangerous and most exciting thing to happen to the planet in longer than I could remember. "I don't know, but he's a trained warrior. Maybe he'll teach us how to fight."

"Us?" My sister laughed. "You're delusional if you think the leaders will let a girl train for battle."

Anger flared within me. "Maybe the Vandar don't have such backward views about the sexes. Maybe he'll let me train."

My sister laughed. "You think the leadership will let him train a female who should be preparing for her betrothal?"

I glared at my sister. "I told you, I'm not marrying *him*."

She shook her head, crossing the room and perching on the edge of her bed across from me. "*He* is the son of one of our ministers, and he's been after you to marry him for ages."

"So?" I shrugged. "Just because Donal wants to marry me, I'm supposed to fall all over myself with gratitude?"

"Marrying a minister's son would be an honor for our family." Her voice was low, but the words hit me like shards of glass. What she meant was that I should be grateful to be considered, considering that our mother was dead, and our father was a worthless drunk.

"Then you marry him."

She gave me a look that made her look much older than her age, and reminded me too much of our mother. "He isn't obsessed with me."

I didn't know why not. Juliette was soft and pretty in a way people on our planet valued, with white-blonde curls falling loose around her shoulders. I was her opposite, wearing my honey-brown hair pulled into a tight bun and trying to avoid male attention. At least, male attention that meant only one thing.

I clenched my teeth, thinking of the minister's son and the arrogant way his gaze roamed my body. "I don't care. I'd rather be alone forever than spend my life with him."

"You know what will happen if you refuse." My sister's voice cracked. "We'll be outcasts, and neither of us will ever be given offers."

I lay on my back staring at the ceiling. Everything my sister said was right, but I couldn't do it. I couldn't be bound to someone who made my skin crawl.

Then my mind drifted to the Vandar who arrived on our planet. Since I'd seen him striding off his ship, his bare chest rippled with muscle and his face set in a menacing scowl, I'd been unable to stop thinking about him. He was so different from the males I'd grown up with. He was clearly a warrior who wouldn't shrink from a challenge.

I clenched my hands in to fists. I was going to convince that Vandar to train me. No matter what it took. I steeled myself. Or what he required in return.

Thank you for reading PURSUED!

If you liked this alien barbarian romance, you'll love PUNISHED, book 5 in the series featuring disgraced Vandar warrior Corvak.

I'm supposed to be in exile on the alien planet, but when I'm asked to help their people defend against my sworn enemy, I can't say no. The human female who begs me to teach her to fight? Her I have to resist—no matter how much she begs or what she offers in return.

One-click PUNISHED Now>

Want to get bonus scenes from all my books and be entered into fun giveaways? Join my VIP Reader group!

https://bit.ly/3lDzLOb

ALSO BY TANA STONE

Raider Warlords of the Vandar Series:

POSSESSED (also available in AUDIO)

PLUNDERED

PILLAGED

PURSUED

PUNISHED

Alien Academy Series:

ROGUE (also available in AUDIO)

The Tribute Brides of the Drexian Warriors Series:

TAMED (also available in AUDIO)

SEIZED (also available in AUDIO)

EXPOSED (also available in AUDIO)

RANSOMED (also available in AUDIO)

FORBIDDEN (also available in AUDIO)

BOUND (also available in AUDIO)

JINGLED (A Holiday Novella)

CRAVED (also available in AUDIO)

STOLEN

SCARRED

The Barbarians of the Sand Planet Series:

BOUNTY (also available in AUDIO)

CAPTIVE (also available in AUDIO)

TORMENT (also available on AUDIO)

TRIBUTE

SAVAGE

CLAIM

TANA STONE books available as audiobooks!

RAIDER WARLORDS OF THE VANDAR:

POSSESSED on AUDIBLE

Alien Academy Series:

ROGUE on AUDIBLE

BARBARIANS OF THE SAND PLANET

BOUNTY on AUDIBLE

CAPTIVE on AUDIBLE

TORMENT on AUDIBLE

TRIBUTE BRIDES OF THE DREXIAN WARRIORS

TAMED on AUDIBLE

SEIZED on AUDIBLE

EXPOSED on AUDIBLE

RANSOMED on AUDIBLE

FORBIDDEN on AUDIBLE

BOUND on AUDIBLE

CRAVED on AUDIBLE

ABOUT THE AUTHOR

Tana Stone is a bestselling sci-fi romance author who loves sexy aliens and independent heroines. Her favorite superhero is Thor (with Aquaman a close second because, well, Jason Momoa), her favorite dessert is key lime pie (okay, fine, *all* pie), and she loves Star Wars and Star Trek equally. She still laments the loss of *Firefly*.

She has one husband, two teenagers, and two neurotic cats. She sometimes wishes she could teleport to a holographic space station like the one in her tribute brides series (or maybe vacation at the oasis with the sand planet barbarians). :-)

She loves hearing from readers! Email her any questions or comments at tana@tanastone.com.

Want to hang out with Tana in her private Facebook group? Join on all the fun at: https://www.facebook.com/groups/tanastonestributes/

Copyright © 2021 by Broadmoor Books

Cover Design by Croci Designs

Editing by Tanya Saari

All rights reserved.

No part of this book may be reproduced in any form or by any electronic or mechanical means, including information storage and retrieval systems, without written permission from the author, except for the use of brief quotations in a book review.

This is a work of fiction. Names, characters, places, and incidents are the products of the author's imagination or are used fictitiously and are not to be construed as real. Any resemblance to actual events, locales, organizations, or persons, living or dead, is entirely coincidental.

Printed in Great Britain
by Amazon